"Aren't you
Holly Grange?"

The voice was as harsh and commanding as the man, the mouth a line of hardness across a face tanned to the color of mahogany. Holly managed a curt nod. How did he know her name, she wondered, glancing wildly around the airport lounge.

"I thought so," the stranger said, "although your photographs don't do you justice." Holly's eyes widened.

"Thank you...I think. And who are you?"

"Bannister." He dropped the word explosively. "Wade Bannister." But it was what followed, which added to the numbing shock that this was her aunt's employer, her host while she was in Australia, that made Holly go pale. "I am, I believe, the rich engineering type you're planning to take for a bundle."

Books by Victoria Gordon

HARLEQUIN ROMANCE

2427—THE SUGAR DRAGON
2433—WOLF AT THE DOOR
2438—THE EVERWHERE MAN
2458—DREAM HOUSE
2469—ALWAYS THE BOSS
2531—DINNER AT WYATT'S
2540—BATTLE OF WILLS
2690—STAG AT BAY
2714—BUSHRANGER'S MOUNTAIN
2727—CYCLONE SEASON

HARLEQUIN PRESENTS

689—BLIND MAN'S BUFF

These books may be available at your local bookseller.

Don't miss any of our special offers. Write to us at the
following address for information on our newest releases.

Harlequin Reader Service
P.O. Box 52040, Phoenix, AZ 85072-2040
Canadian address: P.O. Box 2800, Postal Station A,
5170 Yonge St., Willowdale, Ont. M2N 6J3

Cyclone Season

Victoria Gordon

Harlequin Books

TORONTO • NEW YORK • LONDON
AMSTERDAM • PARIS • SYDNEY • HAMBURG
STOCKHOLM • ATHENS • TOKYO • MILAN

Original hardcover edition published in 1985
by Mills & Boon Limited

ISBN 0-373-02727-3

Harlequin Romance first edition November 1985

CHAPTER ONE

THE sound of the Kalgoorlie flight being announced was, Holly thought, the most marvellous sound she'd heard in years.

'That's it for me then; I'm off,' said her companion, tossing back the remains of a double Scotch as if it were merely water and rising in a welter of luggage to balance precariously on three-inch heels.

'You take care of yourself up north,' said the departing figure. 'And good luck with your engineering type. I hope you take him for a bundle.'

'Oh, I will,' Holly replied, biting back the urge to sigh with relief until after the svelte, slender blonde had left the Perth airport bar.

Then Holly did sigh, and as much in astonishment as relief. Why does this always happen to me, she wondered silently, her ears still ringing with the sound of the blonde's voice. It was a voice she'd been hearing almost non-stop all the way from London, a pleasant enough voice despite the mildly strident Australian accent, but one Holly fervently wished never to hear again.

While she'd been waiting in Customs, it had been a pleasant mental exercise to calculate that she'd been listening to Amanda's sordid history of sex and money for more than twenty hours, but she hadn't—at that point—imagined she'd be in for yet another hour of it.

She'd emerged from Customs to find her own ongoing arrangements completely up in the air and a harassed airline person who could do no more than advise her to wait. The slender blonde had leapt in immediately to drag Holly off to the airport bar. Once there, Holly had been subjected to a quite astonishing lecture on the myraid ways to separate men from their money, their savings, their wives and anything else they possessed.

Too tired and jet-weary to argue, Holly had meekly accepted this continuation of what Amanda had been saying throughout their long journey. In the beginning, she'd sought to stave off the entire conversation by clarifying her own position. She wasn't going to Australia to find a man, not even a rich one. She was merely going on holiday, to see her Aunt Jessica, who was housekeeper to a man who was some sort of mining engineer. From Perth, she'd be flying on northward to Port Hedland.

It was the wrong thing to say. Amanda, it seemed, had 'worked' Port Hedland a few years earlier, and she insisted upon dissecting her experiences in vivid detail for Holly's benefit. By the time they reached Perth, Holly had been informed in equally vivid terms about Amanda's exploits in the opal fields and various other remote mining areas, not only in Australia but overseas as well.

And it was all true! Holly knew that; people didn't lie to Holly. They never had. It was, she thought, due to some strange quirk of her personality, probably the same one that made perfect strangers so eager to relate their life stories to her at the slightest opportunity. The fact that she found it impossible to be rude to anyone didn't help. No matter how much her inner demons would scream at her to call Amanda a gold-digging bitch—which by the blonde's own admission was putting it mildly—Holly found it just couldn't be done.

Amanda wasn't the first, but she was, Holly told herself silently, infinitely the worst. During their hour in the airport bar, she bombarded Holly with instructions on every possible way to use her sexual attractions to financial advantage, prattling on eagerly in blissful ignorance of the fact that Holly wasn't that kind of girl, didn't want to be, and never would be.

'With your looks, you'll knock 'em dead,' the blonde had said. 'That hair . . . and those marvellous eyes . . . and that figure. Wow!'

It might even be true, to a point, although Holly doubted if she looked anywhere near her personal best after more than two days of airplanes and airports and more airplanes. Her mane of dark auburn hair seemed to hang against the slender curve of her neck like something that didn't really belong to her. Her dove-grey eyes felt like they'd been through a desert sandstorm and the part of *that figure* she was most aware of was the numb part on which she sat.

Her mind was equally numb. Even her training as a social worker, training never used because an unexpectedly successful acting career had somehow got in the way, hadn't really prepared Holly for the reality of Amanda, and she found herself struggling through a fog of sheer disbelief for moments after the blonde's departure.

Staring into the remains of the drink she hadn't even really wanted, Holly forced herself to breathe slowly, deeply, as if by that action alone she could fend off the travel weariness that crept through her slender body. When she finally raised her eyes, idly scanning the room around her, it was to find her glance immediately intercepted by the tall, masculine figure at the next table.

Holly met the glance squarely, allowing her features to reveal neither encouragement nor interest. It wasn't unusual for her to be the subject of masculine attention; she'd found that her refreshing, tidy attractiveness had drawn appreciative glances from men ever since she'd been in her mid-teens, and she'd had sufficient time to get used to it by her twenty-sixth birthday.

Except ... this man's glance wasn't, she thought, what could really be termed appreciative. Neutral, even perhaps a shade hostile, she thought, wrenching her eyes away as he rose lithely to his feet.

Oh, no, she thought. The absolute last thing she needed now was to have the problems of discouraging some casual admirer. Amanda, Holly thought, was surely enough to put up with during a single day. Then there was no more time to think; the man was standing over her, a looming, almost predatory figure with a voice to match.

And handsome, although certainly not in any conventional way. There was nothing about him that could be termed anything but hard; he was all planes and angles, starting right from the shock of medium-brown hair that slashed carelessly across his brow. Above eyes like frozen green sea ice were thick, almost beetling brows; below them a nose that looked as if it had been broken and improperly set. His mouth was a line of hardness across a face tanned to the colour of mahogany, and his chin looked as if it had been cleft with an axe.

'It is Holly Grange?' His voice rumbled, burbling up from the broad chest with a curiously ragged resonance. He sounded just like he looked, Holly thought as she managed a curt nod to acknowledge the question.

How could he know her name, she wondered, her mind racing backwards to recall that he'd entered the lounge only moments after she and Amanda, that he must surely have overheard their conversation. Or, rather, Amanda's tedious monologue. But her name? Holly was still struggling to recall if that might have been mentioned when the voice broke through to claim her attention once more.

'I thought so, although I must say your photographs don't do you justice,' the stranger said, and Holly's eyes widened in cautious surprise.

'Thank you ... I think,' she replied. 'But you have the advantage of me, Mr ...'

'Bannister.' He dropped the word explosively. 'Wade Bannister.' But it was what followed, adding to the numbing shock that this was her aunt's employer, her host while she was in Australia, that made Holly's clear, fresh complexion blanch white with shock.

'I am, I believe, the engineering type you're planning to take for a bundle,' Wade Bannister growled, and nothing in the set of his jaw or those icy eyes suggested he found the idea in the slightest way amusing.

Holly swayed, and although she was in no danger of falling from her seat, a massive bronzed hand shot out to catch at her shoulder and steady her. She was held in that grip only for an instant, just long enough to feel as if she were a quail in a bird-dog's mouth, long enough to feel the curious mixture of strength and gentleness. But once she'd steadied, he released her, and that gesture was clearly the type reserved for when one had unexpectedly picked up something distasteful.

'I'd have met you when you got off the plane,' he was saying, voice rumbling through her shock, 'but I was delayed slightly on a business matter ... when I saw you were otherwise occupied, I ...'

'Just thought you'd sit around and eavesdrop a bit,' she interjected sarcastically, the words dripping like acid from her tongue, but nothing compared to the acid that assaulted her pride. What must he have thought? Then, with Amanda's lecture echoing larger-than-life in her ears, Holly knew!

'Oh, my God,' she sighed, 'Oh, but ... but ... No. I know what you must think, and I certainly can't blame you for it, but you're wrong. Quite wrong.'

'Whatever you reckon,' he sighed, and the gesture said far more than the words, to which he then added, 'but now you've got your instructions, I suggest we get moving.'

'Oh, I do wish you'd at least try to understand,' Holly muttered as one enormous hand stretched out to heft her suitcase as if it weighed ounces instead of the scarcely acceptable limit allowed by the airlines. 'And . . . where are we going? I have to tell you that my on-going flight's been cancelled or something.'

'Not cancelled, just postponed,' he growled over his shoulder, not pausing in his stride and clearly expecting Holly to follow him without question.

As they emerged from the terminal into the strong Australian sunlight, Wade Bannister clearly aiming for the car park, Holly suddenly had intense reservations about following him at all. Was he, in fact, her aunt's employer? How could she know he wasn't merely some clever con-man, or criminal, or worse? He might very well have garnered her name from the conversation in the bar, or merely read it from the tag on her luggage.

Holly felt the stirrings of mild panic, then quickened her pace, leaning down to grapple for the handle of her suitcase and then leaning back to halt the tall man's progress.

He stopped, half-turned to face her, those glacial eyes shifting from the suitcase handle they now shared to her own face, now apprehensive, frightened.

'I . . . you . . . just where do you think we're going?' she stammered. 'And, well, how do I know you're who you say you are, even?'

'Do you really doubt it?' And he grinned, but there was no warmth in the grin. 'Still . . . perhaps you've got a point.' And he released the suitcase to reach into one breast pocket, the long, strong fingers emerging with a wallet from which he quickly extracted a driver's licence and then several credit cards, including a bank account identification card with his picture and name clearly exhibited.

'Satisfied?' And again that icy, wolfish grin. He'd already picked up the suitcase again when Holly spoke up.

'No,' she said adamantly. 'No, I'm not. I would like to know where we're going. And why. I was supposed to fly on to Port Hedland in an hour. My Aunt Jessica is expecting me to arrive today and since I can only presume that you have changed my travel arrangements I think it's only fair that you explain why before we go anywhere together.'

Wade Bannister stood silent a moment, his broad-shouldered figure looming so high above her that he provided a sort of living shade.

'Look,' he finally said. 'You're tired and you're suffering from jet-lag. That's for starters. Maybe you're even upset at having your game blown before you even got into the field. I shouldn't be surprised at that, either. But the fact of the matter is that Jessica *isn't* expecting you today; she's expecting you in a few days, after you've had a chance to recover from your trip, after I've had a chance to show you something of Perth . . .'

'But I didn't come here to see Perth. I came to see Aunt Jessica,' Holly interrupted.

'And if it were left to me, I wouldn't be bothered showing you Perth,' was the grating reply, implying silently that he'd rather be showing her nothing but the door of a plane straight back to England. 'But it isn't up to me; I'm following Jessica's wishes in this, and damn it, so will you! Now stop arguing and come along, will you? I've got better things to do than stand around arguing in an airport parking lot.'

Nor did he wait for her reply, but immediately lifted

the suitcase and strode away as if Holly's objections were only a minor, irrelevant aspect of his mission. Holly followed, having to scamper in her medium-heeled shoes to keep up with his long angry strides.

She was panting when they finally reached a sleek, grey Mercedes, into the boot of which her luggage was already being deposited. Wade Bannister, Holly noticed, was even quite deliberately gentle in the way he handled the luggage, but that attitude didn't extend to his treatment of Holly herself.

Sliding into the driver's seat, he leaned over to unlock the passenger door, but made no attempt to help her into the vehicle. Indeed, he hardly waited to see if she could manage the seat belt before sliding the big machine out into the traffic.

He drove in silence and he drove swiftly, easing the car expertly through the highway traffic *en route* to the city centre, where he eventually drew into the underground parking garage of what was obviously a luxury apartment block.

'Home again, home again, jiggedy jig,' he muttered as he turned off the engine, but there was no humour in the remark. Indeed, Holly couldn't even be certain it had been directed at her. Wade didn't bother to hand her out of the car, but merely picked up her luggage and stalked off to the building's entrance, leaving Holly to follow as best she could.

She found him difficult to keep up with, having to almost trot to match his pace, and by the time they'd reached the lifts she was once again short of breath and could feel the perspiration beading at her temples.

Inside the lift, he towered over her, seeming to fill the small compartment with a vital, totally masculine presence of expensive after-shave and sheer bulk. His silence, too, was distinctly overpowering, and Holly found herself stifling a desire to chatter, to somehow break through that wall of silence.

Instead, she contented herself with counting as the lift shot upwards until it stopped at the very top of the building, opening only when Wade brandished a particular key.

Inside, she couldn't help but gasp at the magnificence of the penthouse flat, which was fitted in fine, dark woods and thick, rich carpets. From the lift, they walked straight into a broad entry way-cum-sitting room in which the taste in decoration was distinctly masculine and yet totally correct.

This, Holly sensed, was Wade Bannister's personal domain, classically reflecting his personal tastes and style. And *what* style!

As he escorted her through the massive lounge room and down a hallway with several doors leading off, she realised that this penthouse must take in the entire top floor of the apartment building. It was quite simply the most luxurious accommodation she'd ever seen, so much so that she felt overpowered by the cost factors involved and the power that must be involved in a man who could amass such luxury while still in his early thirties.

'I gather you're impressed,' he said with a sardonic, icy grin. 'It wouldn't have been a bad score, would it?'

Holly flinched as if he'd struck her. Damn the man; would he never give her a chance to explain? Never even so much as consider that what he'd overheard was somebody else talking, not Holly herself?

But he gave her no chance to reply, instead continuing to stride through into a large, airy bedroom with connecting bath. He set down her luggage and turned away immediately, only pausing at the doorway.

'You'll want a shower and then a rest, I reckon,' he said with no hint of friendliness in his voice. 'I'll call you at seven for dinner; we'll talk then.'

'Is there any reason I can't telephone Aunt Jessica, just to let her know I've got this far safely?' Holly asked, and knew the answer before he growled out his reply.

'After we've talked,' he said, and was gone from the room, moving like some great cat, silent on the thick carpet.

Holly stood for a moment, looking at the now-closed door, then shook her head angrily. Autocratic, arrogant bastard, she thought. How dare he treat her like this on the basis of a conversation he didn't understand and didn't choose to even try to understand?

Snatching up her handbag, she flung herself into the hallway and marched swiftly through the flat, her head high and her eyes searching until she eventually found him sprawled in a huge leather chair in the lounge, his suit coat now discarded along with his tie, and a mass of curling dark hair sprouting from the open neck of his whiter-than-white shirt.

'I want to telephone Aunt Jessica and I want to do it now!' Holly proclaimed.

Eyes like green ice raised up from the magazine he'd been holding, surveyed her briefly, contemptuously, she thought, then returned to the magazine.

Holly's anger was fanned by the intentional slur, and she didn't have auburn hair for nothing, despite a lifetime of study on ways to keep one's temper.

'Damn you!' she cried. 'Don't you *dare* treat me as if I didn't exist. I do exist; I'm here and you're going to listen to me whether you like it or not.'

'I thought you were going to have a nap.' The voice was low now, still gravelly and vibrant, but—or did she imagine it—less hostile than before.

'*After* I phone Aunt Jessica,' Holly replied, standing her ground. 'Or is that so much to ask? Surely she might be just a bit worried to know about my arrival.'

'She knows there's no problem. I'd have already phoned her if there was.' His voice was deceptively mild, but Holly knew also that he was lying. This man wouldn't have telephoned her aunt to report a problem—not until it was solved, and therefore no longer relevant.

'She would expect me to phone,' Holly insisted, only to have her argument immediately deflated by his reply.

'I didn't notice you rushing off to phone her when you'd cleared Customs,' he said, scathingly. 'But of course then you'd have had to use your *own* money. Or phoned collect.'

'I certainly would not have,' Holly snapped. 'And what's more, if you were on hand when I cleared Customs you'd know very well that I had to spend nearly twenty minutes trying to sort out the mess *you* created by changing my schedule around. Then, I was going to phone her—and not collect either—but . . .'

'But it was more important to make sure you were totally up to date on the latest, uhm, seduction techniques?' His laugh was bitter, icy, and cruel.

Pride combined with her anger, then, flaring into white-hot rage that wasn't the slightest bit mollified by the fact he was probably quite justified in thinking what he did. Holly's hand lashed out like a striking cat-claw, only be caught by a faster, stronger hand that clamped round her wrist like a steel manacle.

'Don't,' he said, and there was threat in his voice. And warning. And though Holly fought his grip, it was a fruitless, demeaning exercise.

'Let me go!' she spat, grey eyes narrowing in anger that had lost its white fury but was still bitter.

'Only when you promise to behave,' he shrugged, but an instant later released her wrist without waiting for any verbal promise.

Trembling still in her anger, Holly rubbed at her

wrist before plunging it into her handbag, scrabbling furiously through her wallet until she'd selected the entirety of her Australian currency.

'There, damn it,' she cried, flinging the sheaf of bills at Wade and heedless that they fanned into a shower that had no impact upon reaching him. 'If it's money you're worried about, then that settles it. Now I'm either going to phone Aunt Jessica from here, or I'm damned well going somewhere where I can phone her. Is that understood?'

'Interesting, anyway,' he shrugged, making no attempt to pick up the money. 'But then you *are* supposed to be something of an actress, aren't you? Which of your performances is this particular scenario from?'

'It's from the scenario that includes *goodbye!*' Holly said in a voice so calm she could scarce believe it was her own. Her body was less calm; as she knelt to pick up the scattered money, her fingers trembled and her balance seemed strangely precarious. But eventually she managed it, and rose shakily to her feet.

'I'm sorry, Mr Bannister, that your eavesdropping has led you to such a total misunderstanding,' she whispered, keeping her voice as calm as her ragged breathing would allow. 'I can understand why you think as you do, but I'm equally sure that—given any sort of fair opportunity—I could explain things. Obviously, however, that won't be possible, so I think it's best that we part company here and now.'

'Ah? With you going where?' His own voice was fearfully, maddeningly calm and he showed none of the trauma that now threatened to rip Holly apart. She hated confrontation of any kind; this man seemed to thrive on it.

'Anywhere,' Holly replied shakily, 'that I can be treated like a normal human being, that I can be allowed to show normal consideration by telephoning my aunt, and that I don't have to endure your arrogant, sneering attitudes.'

'You can telephone your aunt after dinner, after we've talked,' he replied quietly. 'Now, you're tired and you're starting to get cranky.' And now his tones were those normally reserved for recalcitrant five-year-olds. 'So why don't you go have a nap and then we'll have dinner and perhaps you'll feel better.'

'I will *not* feel better and I will *not* have a nap!' Holly snapped, horrified inside to hear herself speaking exactly as the child he'd been speaking to. She could feel the tears welling up to her wide grey eyes, and she squinched them shut to hold back the final, devestating sign of her defeat.

'Well you won't do much else. The door's locked and I've got the key; the phone's locked up and I've got that key too,' he replied, infuriating. 'So why don't you just try doing what you're asked, for once?'

It was the final straw. From somewhere inside came a final vestige of angry strength, desperate strength; unthinkingly Holly flung herself at him, reacting only to her anger and to his bitter condescension.

The impact of Holly's assault forced Wade back in the wide lounge chair, but even as her fingers scrabbled across his broad chest, his arms were closing around her, confining her with maddening ease.

She butted with her head, trying to strike him, then clawed with her fingers, her legs kicking, her entire body involved in the assault. To no avail. He held her as easily as if she'd been a child, oblivious to her cries of frustration and rage.

Held her, manoeuvred her gradually until she was sprawled half across his lap. One arm was pinioned between her body and his. He held the other arm imprisoned with one hand, and when his voice reached her, it seemed rather more incredulous than just angry. 'What in blazes do you think you're doing?' he asked.

'Oh, God, but I hate you,' Holly spat, writhing in another futile gesture to free herself, oblivious to the fact that her every movement pushed her skirt higher on her thighs, brought her entire body somehow closer to him.

'And so you should,' he muttered softly, almost endearingly. 'So you should.' His lips as he spoke were brushing against the softness of her hair, the arm around her somehow took on an element not of imprisonment, but of intimacy.

Startled by her instinctive and unexpected response to the caress, she could only stare at him wide-eyed as his lips swooped to claim her mouth, his pale eyes locking her glance with hypnotic effectiveness as their mouths met.

Holly struggled, but now the fight was more with herself than with Wade Bannister. Never had she been so totally, so suddenly aroused. Her entire body seemed to mould itself to his, ignoring the commands of her mind. His lips were first harsh, then soft, searching, devouring, demanding from her a response that she couldn't accept, yet couldn't ignore.

His arm around her shoulders supported her, but his hand, in cupping the nape of her neck, sent shivers of ecstasy down her spine. Her own hand, lifted to strike at him, to claw her way free, instead circled his neck, her fingers exploring in the thickness of his hair, her wrist alive to the play of his muscles against her pulse.

When his free hand touched her throat it was bliss, when his fingers roamed down the hollows of her shoulder to the soft roundness of her breast, she found herself breathless with the wonder of his touch. And when it moved still lower, exploring expertly the curves of knee and thigh, she couldn't keep herself from twisting passionately to ease its passage beneath her clothing. It was as if their bodies were fused by some magical electrical charge. All the curves fitted, all the contours were complementary.

And all the fight was gone from Holly. She could no longer deny the impossible demands of her body, the screams of protest from her conscious mind. All she wanted was more of this man's lovemaking.

His fingers were instruments of tortuous pleasure, playing upon her nerve endings with practised skill until her entire body cried out for more. Her body, but not her mind. In a final burst of logic, of sanity, she tore her lips from his, crying out.

'No ... oh please, no. No more.'

Whereupon he thrust her from him, eyes burning with glacial fire as he stared down at her. 'Yes,' he said abruptly. 'I suppose this isn't really the proper way to discipline you, is it?'

Her ears heard him, her mind caught the message with bitter clarity, but even after she'd fled the room in ignominious flight, her body still cried out for him over the sound of her bedroom door slamming behind her and the wailing of her tears as she flung herself on to the bed and collapsed.

But when he knocked softly at her door an hour—or was it many hours—later, Holly had no difficulty in meeting his eyes with a gaze of her own that was appropriately cold.

Bastard! Her mind screamed the accusation silently, her heart denied it and yet raged with abused feelings at the same time. And on the surface she was chillingly polite, totally in control now despite the seething turmoil inside.

'We should go down for dinner soon,' he said gently, making no reference to the earlier episode. 'If I give you half an hour will it be enough?'

'I'm ready now,' she replied steadily. She wasn't; she looked awful and felt worse, but damned if she'd trouble to make herself beautiful for this arrogant so-and-so.

'Suit yourself,' he replied with a trace of embarrassment. 'But I'm going to have a shower and change, and I'd suggest you do the same, because you certainly don't look your best, and if you don't mind me saying so, you smell like the inside of an airplane.'

And to Holly's astonishment he grinned boyishly after making the statement, the smile lighting up his eyes and face with a gentleness that demolished her own anger.

She looked down at her crumpled travelling clothes, now the worse for having been slept in, and shook her head. 'I suppose you're right,' she admitted, knowing that her own pride, her own sense of self-worth, wouldn't allow her to be seen in public looking like *this*.

'Good,' he said, voice still gentle, eyes still warm. 'There's a hair-dryer in your bathroom, and most anything else you might need, and there's no real hurry. The restaurant here won't be all that crowded midweek, and they know we're coming.'

For just an instant, rebellion flared. Then Holly let her common sense prevail. So what if this tall, changeable man could command changes in airline flights and restaurant bookings at will? Could command, it seemed, herself at will, also? He was Jessica's friend and employer, and if changing for dinner brought Holly any closer to resolving the tension between them, it was a small price to pay.

'Shall I need to be very dressed up?' she asked then, knowing, somehow, that it was a silly question. For anything less, Wade Bannister wouldn't be changing; his immaculate business suit had suffered far less than her own travel gear during their earlier tussle.

He smiled again, and Holly found herself unable to escape the comparison between this smiling man and the cold-eyed rake who'd so thoroughly rejected her before.

'It might be nice, considering we'll be celebrating your arrival in Australia,' he said then. 'I'm sure you'll have something suitable.'

And he turned away, still with a friendly smile that belied Holly's immediate suspicion that he was having a go at her. She watched the door close behind him, then flung off her clothes and revelled in the steamy warmth of the shower, emerging to find a surprising stock of feminine cosmetics—all new and unopened—and the promised hair-dryer.

Deciding what to wear, once her luxuriant mane of auburn hair was dried to a shimmering, flattering style, was both problem and no problem at all. Jessica's written descriptions of Port Hedland hadn't indicated much need for posh clothing, so everything Holly had brought, bar one single garment, was designed for casual leisure wear or travel. The only dress she had that would be suitable for this evening was far too provocative for the mood she found herself in just now.

It was floor-length, exactly the soft grey of her eyes, and featured a keyhole neckline that combined modesty and sensuality with its high collar and low-cut and far too revealing keyhole for the image she wanted to project.

Worse, because the dress required a special-fitting bra that she'd somehow forgotten to pack, she'd be forced to wear it without one. Not a pleasant prospect, she thought.

She knew only too well that Wade Bannister would notice the lack as quickly as he'd notice the fact that the skirt was slit to mid-thigh on both sides to ease the snugness of the overall fit. He'd notice, but hopefully wouldn't put the worst possible implication on her choice. Maybe.

When she emerged from her room, treading lightly in the high heels the dress necessitated, Holly found herself strangely reticent about making any sort of entrance. When she peered round a corner to discover Wade Bannister, resplendent in traditional evening wear, she was torn between being glad of her limited choice of garment and being stirred by just how amazingly attractive her host was.

The dinner jacket he wore fitted perfectly, as did everything else. Clearly he didn't buy his dress clothes off the rack, and looking at the breadth of his shoulders, the narrowness of his hips, and the length of his long, muscular legs, she could partially imagine why. But it wasn't only size that made this man choose hand-tailored clothes, Holly knew. His car, his apartment, his very deportment indicated that he worked to have the best and chose it with an innate good taste.

'I hope I've not been too long,' she said, feeling the words stick in her throat as she walked uncertainly into the lounge room and saw him turn to survey her. But if she'd expected anything, it certainly wasn't the slow smile and very definite nod of approval.

'Exquisite,' he breathed in a voice like silk, and to her surprise stepped forward to lift her hand to his lips in a gesture so natural to him that she couldn't even think to be fearful of it.

'We've still time for a quick drink, if you like,' he said then. 'Would you like sherry, or prefer something stronger?'

'Something soft would suit me best, actually,' she replied, thrilling to his glance, his touch, and yet wishing he would be less attentive, less aware of the fact that she hadn't worn a bra and that her long legs were displayed expertly by the gown she wore.

He smiled, saying, 'Whatever suits you,' and opened an exquisite antique drinks cabinet to produce a wide array of bottles and glasses.

'You ... uhm ... you mentioned that we had to talk,' she began tentatively after accepting the drink he offered. But then she faltered totally as he put a finger to his lips and then—with a genuinely friendly grin—whispered, 'Not on an empty stomach.'

Moments later they were descending in the lift, to emerge on what Holly presumed was the public floor of the huge building, and to her surprise it was a floor fully equipped with various shops and a restaurant that even to her inexperienced eye fairly shouted its exclusivity.

Wade took her arm as they entered the restaurant, and continued to hold it as they walked through the reception area where a tall, slender hostess escorted them to their table with a graciousness reserved for Wade alone. Holly got only the envious glance she recognised as the fate of any woman found in this man's company.

They dined on enormous king prawns and oysters Kilpatrick and huge, Western Australian crayfish, helping the seafood down with quantities of a wine Holly had never heard of, but which was ambrosia to her parched throat.

And they talked, but of nothing consequential. They talked of Holly's journey, of her life before coming to Australia, even briefly of Wade's work and the various attractions of Perth they'd have to investigate before heading north.

Wade was courtesy itself. He seemed to have decided that what Holly needed was relaxed conversation, and he set out to relax her and did it with style and charm.

The food, the surroundings, lost significance. Her mind was almost totally preoccupied with the startling betrayal of her body. It was a shattering revelation to find that not only could he charm her, but that in the relaxed atmosphere he so deliberately created, her body was responding to him.

Each movement of his hands, hands that she now knew could stir her body to sensuous delights undreamt of even in her wildest fantasies, was enough to keep her stomach aflutter. When he looked at her—and while there was no true affection in his glance there was also no hostility—she could feel her nipples hardening, her entire skin seeming to glow.

It was insane! Nowhere in any sociology book, nor in her personal experience of the opposite sex, was there anything to have prepared her for the incredible physical attraction Wade Bannister could exert on her without even seeming to try.

And if he did try? Holly tried not to think about that, but her efforts were futile. She could hardly think of anything else. And it was marvellous, a truly delightful evening.

Until the coffee and liqueurs arrived, and he said, without any warning at all, 'Now, where's this explanation you've been waiting to offer me?'

Holly was taken totally by surprise, exactly as she realised immediately he'd intended, but she was also rested now, and no longer quite so afraid of him, despite being so attracted. So she paused only a second before explaining to him briefly the circumstance of her meeting with Amanda, her predilection for attracting total strangers, and the ensuing conversation he'd overheard.

Strangely enough, he listened well, not interrupting until she'd finished, and not showing by so much as a raised eyebrow whether he was believing her or not. Then he made a single, straight-to-the-heart-of-it-all comment and destroyed her every illusion that she might have convinced him.

'Quote,' he said. 'Word for word and I've got a very, very good memory: She said "I hope you take him for a bundle," and you replied, "Oh, I will." Correct?'

'Correct,' Holly agreed, 'although why you should imagine I'd see any sense in arguing with her at that point, I can't think.'

'Call it a sense of self-preservation,' Wade replied grimly, but then softened his reply with a smile. And Holly noticed that it was a proper smile, a genuine smile. 'But okay, I'll give you the benefit of the doubt. It isn't really terribly significant when you consider that I'm not looking for a wife or ... whatever ... anyway, and that we have more significant things to worry about just now.'

'I don't follow you,' Holly said, torn between the urge to rage out at him for not accepting her story verbatim and the sense of real caution his attitude now provoked.

'Well, whatever else. I think I must accept that you really do, honestly, care for your aunt,' he said, not really making it a question, but putting sufficient inflexion into the words that Holly immediately snapped a response.

'I would think that rather obvious,' she snapped, 'and I, at least, wouldn't think of questioning your own concern, ignoring what you might think of me.'

'I don't know, yet, just what I think of you, except that I wasn't lying when I said your pictures don't do you justice,' he replied. Not angrily, but he wasn't soft anymore, either.

But then he did soften. It was obvious in his glance, his very demeanour. 'She's not a well woman, Jessica,' he said, and Holly could see the concern, the genuine concern. 'And it would be best, whatever *we* think, if when we arrive in Port Hedland she thinks we're at least ...'

'At least what?' Holly finally had to demand. He'd left the sentence hanging in mid-air, but with something, some undercurrent that left her rigidly alert, cautious.

He grinned, and it was that infuriating grin of a ten-year-old with a secret. 'It's ... a bit tricky to explain without you blowing your top, especially under the circumstances. Let's just say it's rather important to Jessica that we, uhm, like each other.'

Holly's stomach flip-flopped as realisation struck her. It couldn't be true—it mustn't. She could handle almost anything, especially for the sake of her aunt's health, but ... this? Her voice was squeaky when she finally got out the words. 'Like each other—just exactly how?'

'Oh, I think you can figure it out easily enough,' he replied, and this time his grin was genuinely rueful.

'She's been matchmaking!' Holly spat out the obvious truth as if it left a bad taste in her mouth. No wonder this man had been so put out at her apparent style. What a jolt it must have been to find himself matched with a ... a ... gold-digger. Or worse, she thought, but couldn't admit to the word for it.

Then she caught Wade's glance and realised she was only half right. That the truth was far more involved and far more convoluted than she had ever begun to imagine.

And—silently, because out loud would be worse than a waste of time—she wished Amanda dead.

CHAPTER TWO

'It's worse than just matchmaking, isn't it?' she heard
herself asking in a small, almost childlike voice. And
dreading the answer. 'She's convinced herself that the
match has already been made, hasn't she?'

Wade's glance was a curious mixture of sympathy
and sternness. Not that she could expect much else,
Holly thought. What a shock his eavesdropping must
have been! Bad enough to know he was the—
unwilling?—half of a matchmaking venture by some
woman he truly cared for, but to find the other half
was—or at least appeared—little better than a
whore . . .

'Well then she'll just have to think again, won't she,'
Holly said. 'Because while I think we might—just
might—be able to conceal our mutual antipathy, I can't
imagine either of us being good enough at acting to
carry off the impression of anything more . . .'

'Intimate?' he said when she found her tongue
twisting and unable to finish a simple statement. And
his eyes were alight now with an unholy glow that made
Holly distinctly wary. That single word, just the way
he'd said it, was enough to touch her body like a caress,
and she hated herself for her reaction.

'Mutual antipathy is, I'd suggest, putting it much too
strong, but intimate . . . well . . . I thought you put on a
rather good performance of that earlier today,' he said,
and quite without warning reached out to take her hand.

Holly never had a chance. She tried to retract her
hand, but his lean fingers held her captive while his
thumb stroked idly at the racing pulse in her wrist.

'And it was an act, of course,' he said rather musingly. 'My, what a strange girl you are. You talked so far from innocence, there with your tarty friend at the airport, but you can put on a blush without even trying, or tears, or even a fit of trembling. Makes me wonder which was really the act, and if you, yourself, really know.'

And he laughed, softly, but it seemed cruel, barbed laughter that tore at Holly's composure, wounding her as effectively as he did with his caressing, deceitful fingers.

'Damn you,' she whispered, trying vainly to pull away her hand, yet inwardly wishing it could stay in his grasp forever.

'Why?' he whispered in return. 'For turning you on? And don't bother to deny it; your pulse is racing like wildfire.'

'That's anger, not being turned on,' she lied, trying again to snatch her hand free. 'You, of all people, should know that nothing you do is likely to turn me on. Mutual antipathy . . . remember?'

'I remember,' he said with an enigmatic glance. 'But will you? Maybe we'll have to see about that, later.' And her heart sank with the sudden realisation of where she'd be spending that night. Alone . . . in a private flat to which only Wade Bannister held the key.

'Let's not bother,' she sneered as convincingly as she knew how. 'I'm sure even Aunt Jessica would draw the line someplace in her illusions. At least, I wish she had.'

'As do I,' he muttered, and released her wrist so suddenly that Holly practically felt the ice, the contempt.

But then, to her utter surprise, he burst into laughter. And it was genuine laughter, not staged and not filled with the bitterness she might have expected. 'Poor old Jess,' he chuckled. 'So many dreams, but forgetting there were real people behind them with a . . . mutual antipathy. It's a bit sad, really. But then,' and now his eyes were hard, cold with the seriousness of his thoughts, 'I suppose we'll just have to let her down as gently as we can. Who knows, by the time we've collaborated that long we might actually get along.'

Then warning flags went up behind his eyes, but Holly leapt into the breach with an immediate demand for more information. 'Just how bad is it?' she cried softly. 'What, exactly, is Jessica going to expect from us?'

'A lot more compatibility than either of us seems able to muster,' was his reply, placid and yet somehow definite, firm.

'And you're positive that she wouldn't accept that we're just not compatible?'

'Positive,' he replied without hesitation. 'Especially because based on everything she knows—or thinks she knows—we ought to be very compatible.'

'Which is something she couldn't possibly have determined without a lot of help from you,' Holly guessed out loud. And had to stop herself from verbalising a regret that he'd shown up late at the airport, that he'd overheard a conversation—a monologue, really—that could give him nothing but the most unfair and worst of impressions.

Wade shrugged, the gesture that nebulous type that could have meant anything at all. 'We did talk about you a fair bit, or at least Jessica did. All I ever did was honestly say that I thought your pictures showed you must be a very attractive young woman; she took it from there.'

Holly could have cried. What a horrible mistake, what a useless mistake, she thought. If only she'd known, but she hadn't, and perhaps it was best this way. Meeting Wade Bannister on her aunt's terms, she might have fallen all too easily into the still-ready trap.

'Well, what do you propose to do about it?' she demanded peevishly. And when he didn't answer immediately, seeming to be lost in thoughts of his own, a sudden rush of vengeful brilliance occurred to her. It was perfect, the more so because it might ensure that he'd leave her alone, permanently.

'Maybe we should just get married on the way to the airport,' she said brightly, and had the satisfaction—the immense satisfaction—of seeing him blanch at the thought. It was only for a second, but Holly knew she'd struck a nerve as surely as if she'd used a dentist's drill on him.

'I really think it would suffice if we could appear just reasonably friendly,' he said, the words sliding through clenched teeth. 'Even your Aunt Jessica can't be expecting miracles.'

'Oh, but think how pleased she'd be,' Holly cooed, twisting the knife deeper and savouring every evidence of Wade's discomfort.

'Stop it.' The command in his voice was unmistakable, but Holly was past caring. She had the bit in her teeth now, and she was going for broke.

'Of course, she'd be devastated at missing the wedding, so maybe we'd best have her fly down for it,' she mused, hiding her inward smile behind glittering, liquid grey eyes. 'You could afford that, surely?'

'I said stop it, and I meant it,' he said in a voice as cold as death.

'No, why should I?' Holly retorted. 'You can't have it both ways, and if you won't stop treating me like a . . . like a . . . whore, then you can't complain if I act like one, can you?'

'I've already said I'd give you the benefit of the doubt, and certainly you can't say I've treated you like a . . . like that tonight,' he replied, still cool, still without ever showing that he might be under the slightest pressure.

'Benefit of the doubt—fiddlesticks!' Holly retorted. 'You haven't even thought of accepting my explanation and frankly I doubt if you ever will, so what's the point of continuing this charade? It's perfectly obvious you and I can't even be decently civil to one another, let alone fool Jessica into thinking we might actually like one another.'

'Her, and more than her,' he growled, with a curious little grin and his ice green eyes directed in such a fashion that warned Holly his attention was now looking somewhere beyond her.

A smart remark rose to her lips, but the feminine voice Holly heard wasn't her own. It was a brittle yet very, very sensuous voice that arrived from behind her in words of genuine greeting for Wade Bannister, who was already rising to greet the newcomer.

And his reply to the greeting was especially warm, revealed in a genuine smile and twinkling eyes that instantly lost all the icy chill Holly seemed to put there.

'This is a surprise. I thought you were still flitting about in Singapore.' He smiled in welcome to the slender, lovely blonde who followed her own words into view.

'And I thought you were busy collecting your housekeeper's little niece,' was the reply, followed by a glance at Holly that whirled through alarm, assessment and dismissal within the flicker of one haughty eyebrow.

Even after the formalities of an introduction, Ramona Mason did her best to ignore Holly's presence, although the blonde's attitude admitted mild curiosity when informed that Holly was the *little* niece in question.

Ramona obviously had eyes only for Wade Bannister, and once he'd seated her at their table and ordered her drink, she did her very best to freeze Holly out entirely.

Which should have been just fine, but for some reason it wasn't. Being studiously ignored by the brittle blonde was almost as bad as being patronised, Holly thought. Not that she cared a fig for Wade's taste in women; it was nothing to do with her, after all.

Ramona, apparently, had come in to finalise the arrangements for a dinner party the following evening, and upon learning that Wade wouldn't be flying north until the day after that, she promptly invited him to attend.

'I won't promise but to try,' he replied. 'I've got a lot of business to attend to tomorrow, but if I can get through it, and if Holly doesn't succumb to the dreaded jet-lag, we'd love to come.'

'You'll be here, then,' Ramona cooed. 'I've never known business to keep you from a good party, and even if Miss Grange isn't up to it, that's no reason for you not to attend.'

Holly translated that to mean that she hadn't been included in the invitation anyway, and that she'd likely be wise to feign jet-lag or exhaustion, because this woman didn't want her at the party—she wanted Wade Bannister all to herself.

'I shan't be able to go with you, of course,' Holly said a moment later, after Ramona had—thankfully—taken her leave.

'And I suppose you've got some quite logical reason for that remark,' Wade replied. 'But isn't it a bit early to decide?'

'Not at all. In the first place, she didn't really include me in the invitation; even you could see that, I'm sure. Also, I've nothing to wear, as this dress is the only thing remotely suitable that I brought with me.'

'And of course you couldn't wear that, because Ramona's seen it, and with stirling feminine logic that puts it out of bounds, or something equally ridiculous,' he scoffed.

'Something like that,' Holly replied. Let him think what he pleased; she didn't want to be a fifth wheel at the party and would find any plausible excuse for not attending.

'Well, since I'd be wearing the same thing as tonight, I can't imagine why you couldn't do the same,' he said. 'That outfit is, to say the very least, suitable, and wearing it you'd have every other woman in the place green with envy, just as you've done tonight.'

'The only green eyes in the place tonight are yours,' Holly jibed, knowing but not daring to say that if there was envy involved, it was because of her companion, not her dress.

'Ah, but not with envy,' Wade replied with a smile. 'Yours, on the other hand, are showing definite signs of sleepiness, so I suggest we trot back up to the flat, phone dear Jessica, and then if you're very good I'll tuck you into bed.'

'You'll do no such thing,' Holly retorted, savagely wishing he couldn't make her heart do flip-flops with a simple comment like that. Not, at least, by making it deliberately to provoke her.

'Why, I wonder,' Wade replied musingly, his eyes gleaming with mocking lights that belied the softness of his voice. 'Is it because you have no intention of being very good? Or . . .'

'Because I'm quite capable of tucking myself into bed, without any help at all from you, whether I'm good or not,' she stated firmly. 'I will, however, very definitely accept your suggestion that we call Aunt Jessica, because regardless of your earlier assurances, I've been feeling guilty about not telephoning her immediately I got off the plane.'

'You do, however, accept that I was right in delaying the call under the circumstances?' he asked. 'I did think it was best that we reached some sort of agreement before you spoke to her; at least now you'll know what to expect.'

'I know what your interpretation is,' Holly hedged. 'It wouldn't surprise me to find out that you've over-reacted a great deal to what might be no more than a natural hope that we'll ... well ... get along, anyway. After all, in visiting Aunt Jessica I'm making myself, really, a guest in your home.'

'Which, having decided for yourself that we're quite, uhm, incompatible, doesn't please you one little bit, does it?' Wade asked abruptly.

'I would feel a great deal better about it if we hadn't got off to such a bad start,' Holly admitted.

'Hardly my fault, though, was it?' he replied. 'The worst I did was to arrive a bit late at the airport.'

'And then spend your time eavesdropping and putting your own totally wrong interpretations on what you heard.'

'I thought we'd already settled that,' he replied, no longer quite so friendly. 'You've explained, and I've accepted that explanation; you couldn't ask for more than that.'

'You *say* you've accepted it,' Holly replied.

'I don't usually say things I don't mean,' he said. 'Why are you so determined at this particular moment to make a new issue of it? Or can't you face up to Jessica's matchmaking tactics without somehow shoving the blame on to me?'

'I can't face up to them, period.' Holly replied. 'After all, I've not seen Jessica since I was ten years old. She only knows me from my letters and the occasional telephone call. How could she *make* such assumptions?'

Wade seemed hardly moved. 'She's not getting any younger,' he said. 'And though it may be hard to understand from your youthful point of view, people who are getting on in years often entertain rather exotic whims about people they care for.'

'Oh, stop being so damned logical,' Holly snapped.

'Only if *you'll* start,' he replied. 'For God's sake, woman, nobody's asking you to throw yourself at my feet or anything like that. Just that we try and get along. Jessica's going in for a series of tests tomorrow, and I want her in the most relaxed, happy state possible.

'Which means,' he continued ominously, 'that she doesn't twig to the fact either of us knows she's going for the tests, or even that she's not top of the world. And that she thinks we're enjoying each other's company here in Perth so she can sneak in and out of hospital, as she's been doing for the past year, with the firm conviction that she's worrying nobody but herself.'

Holly was aghast. 'Do you mean to tell me she's been keeping her ill-health a secret? Even from you? I mean, well, I could understand it in my case, being so far away, but you? Surely she'd realise you'd have to notice sooner or later.'

'Being typically female, she's capable of believing just exactly what she wants to believe,' he shrugged. 'Or maybe she just reckons I'm stupid; I don't know. And frankly, I don't much care. If her little deceptions make her happy, or make it easier for her to cope with the problem, then who am I to rain on her parade?'

'You really care for her, don't you?' Holly asked softly, knowing the answer, but asking anyway.

'She is the closest thing I've had to a mother since my own died many years ago,' he replied. 'And quite the finest woman I've ever met since I was old enough to tell good from bad. If she was twenty years younger and would have had me—which I rather doubt—I'd have married her years ago.'

Holly didn't reply to that statement. What, indeed,

could she have said? A moment later, any chance she might have had disappeared.

'Therefore, dear Holly, if she wants us to be compatible, we will be compatible! Is that now perfectly clear?'

'Perfectly,' Holly muttered, and being slightly miffed by the new arrogance, the strength of command in his voice, she added under her breath, 'I just hope she doesn't decide we ought to be married, while she's at it.'

'Not even for Jessica would I go that far,' Wade growled, 'but we will be friendly and happy and comfortable together if I have to paddle your pretty little undercarriage twice a day to make sure you keep it in mind.'

'Personally, I think you'd accomplish more by just being reasonable yourself,' she replied staunchly. 'I don't react terribly well to being threatened.'

'That was a promise, not a threat,' he replied. 'But I take your point. Now let's get this phone call out of the way.'

Five minutes later they were in the office portion of Wade's flat, he with telephone in hand and a wry expression playing round that bold, expressive mouth. Holly's stomach was busy playing hop-scotch, but Wade seemed calm as anything while he waited for his connection.

'Jess? Everything okay at home?' he said, then. 'Good, because I have this rather lovely young world traveller here who says she's related to you. I'll let you speak to her in a moment, but first I want to ask if you'll insist she go out and buy a new dress tomorrow because we've been invited to a posh party tomorrow night and she keeps insisting the dress she's wearing at the moment isn't suitable, or some such thing.'

He paused, listening to something Jessica was saying but winking mischievously at Holly's furious frown.

'It would be hard to imagine her in anything more flattering,' he said then. And his eyes raked across Holly's figure in a glance that floated between caress and naked lust. 'If this is what jet-lag does to her, she ought to fly more often. But that's beside the point; I know she's dying to speak to you, so I'll put her on now. Hang on.'

He handed over the phone to Holly, who found it necessary to turn away from him. Not for reasons of privacy, but because he insisted on continuing that visual caress, and she knew it would be impossible to keep the effect of his appraisal from her own voice. It was almost exactly as if he'd really been touching her.

'Sounds like you've made quite an impression,' Aunt Jessica chuckled as soon as they were through the formalities of greeting. 'And what do you think of him?'

Oh, Lord, thought Holly. He was right and worse than right. Jessica is matchmaking with a bold hand indeed. Her thoughts didn't make a reply any easier.

'Uhm ... interesting,' she finally managed to say, praying that it was a sufficiently nebulous answer to satisfy Jessica without saying too much to Wade Bannister. Damn Jessica anyway; what kind of answers could she expect, knowing full well the object of the discussion was sitting only inches from Holly. And eavesdropping, as usual.

'That isn't much of an answer,' Jessica said. 'The kind of thing one says while trying to avoid saying something less complimentary.'

'Oh, it was a good trip. A bit tiring, but I was able to arrange layovers here and there, so I arrived in fairly good shape,' Holly said, deliberately changing the subject. She would *not* talk about Wade Bannister while he was sitting right behind her. Indeed, she wouldn't talk about him anyway, given any choice in the matter. Unfortunately, there was little if any chance of that.

'Oh, all right. I get the message,' her aunt said. 'So when are you flying home here? I want to be sure and meet the plane, don't forget.'

'I'm . . . I'm not sure,' Holly found herself admitting. 'Mr Bannister has apparently made all the arrangements, so I'll just put him back on, if you like.'

'The plane gets in at two in the afternoon; not tomorrow, mind, but the day after,' he said, then paused while Holly repeated the instructions.

'All right, Holly dear. I'll be waiting. And please tell Wade that everything's just fine, here. He's inclined to worry about me sometimes, especially when he's away for long periods.'

'I'll . . . tell him,' Holly said. 'Goodbye for now and I'll see you when our flight gets in.'

'So,' Wade said with a sober, almost harsh expression once she'd hung up the telephone, 'I'm merely *interesting*, am I? Really, I'd have thought you might do better than that. After all, I fairly raved about you.'

'I wasn't speaking about you when I said that,' Holly lied. 'I was talking about my trip.'

'Bulldust! Which, if you need it translated, means . . .'

'I know what it means, or at least I can guess,' Holly said. 'And all right, so I *was* talking about you. What else could you expect me to say with you sitting there breathing down my neck?'

'Oh . . . handsome, charming, debonair; or rough, tough and nasty; big, bad, bold and expensive. Something a little more daring than just *interesting*. I can see, dear Holly, that I'll have to set about making more of an impression on you than I have so far.'

Then he grinned wolfishly. 'And just for the record, I wasn't breathing down your neck; I was studying that most astonishingly lovely back and thinking that when you're tense, you develop the most interesting dimples just about here . . .'

'Keep your hands to yourself!' Holly snapped, swivelling out of his reach. 'If you want to play those kind of games, I can think of somebody who'd be more than willing to join you I'm sure. But it isn't me.'

'My, my. Instant antipathy in my case, and instant jealousy elsewhere. You're certainly one for the first impressions, aren't you, dear Holly?'

'Not as a general rule. And just for *your* record, I am not *dear* Holly,' she replied.

'Judging from the way your temperament is coming all unstuck, I'd say you're close to being a very jet-lagged Holly,' Wade replied, apparently nonplussed at her hostility.

So much so, that he grinned very engagingly at her before saying, 'Which isn't really that surprising, considering the strain of the past few days. So it's off to bed with you, I think, and don't be a bit surprised if you sleep 'till noon because you may very well need it. Just so long as you're up in time to go buy that new dress.'

'I am not buying any new dress,' Holly avowed. 'In fact, the way I feel just now, I'll still be sound asleep when you're off enjoying that party much more without me.'

'And have to explain to Jess why I left you all alone and went off to the party without you? Oh, no. You'll be there—in this dress, which I think I'd prefer, or a new one. But you will be there, dear Holly, if I have to drag you kicking and screaming.'

And she was, complete with new dress. In fact, Holly's only satisfaction stemmed from the dress, and that didn't last long. She had indeed slept until noon. Until one-thirty, actually, when she woke startled—at first—then merely ravenous. She rose, threw on her wrap and slipped out of her bedroom to see if Wade was still present in the flat.

To her great pleasure, he wasn't, but he'd left a note for her, prominently displayed on the refrigerator door.

Afternoon, sleepyhead. You'll have to go out for brekkie because I ate all that was here and it'll be lunch time by then anyway. I can recommend the *Golden Eagle* if you like Chinese, or *Luis*' if you're feeling more traditional. Should be back in time for the party at eight. Don't forget the dress! And I've left you some cash in case you need it.

The message wasn't signed, not that it could have come from anyone but Wade. Holly stood there, staring at it for a moment, then opened the envelope attached and stared even wider when she saw his idea of *some* cash.

'What does he expect me to do—buy the entire dress shop?' she muttered to herself. Not that it mattered what Wade might expect; Holly knew she'd not spend a penny of his money on a dress. Or even on lunch, for that matter. She had enough of her own and plenty of traveller's cheques.

Besides, she wasn't going to buy a dress, because she wasn't going to get roped into attending the party. Not if she could help it.

By the time she'd showered and dressed, however, reason had more or less returned, and she knew that her feelings for Jessica would end up giving Wade the lever he needed to keep her in line—within reason. Unfortunately, buying a dress and going to a party, even one thrown by Ramona Mason, could hardly be described as unreasonable.

She spent the rest of the afternoon wandering the city streets of Perth and marvelling at the wisdom of the city's early planners. The location on the Swan River couldn't be faulted, and the tourist map she procured showed just how the beauty spots of the river had been emphasised in the overall plan.

She spent a pleasant hour in the museum and art gallery, wishing it could be more like a pleasant three days, just to see everything properly. Lunch ignored the restaurants Wade had suggested in favour of bits and pieces picked up from small street stalls and milk bars.

And although she had to fight with herself about it, Holly kept an eye out as she passed various dress shops and boutiques, although it was late afternoon before she found *the* dress.

It was in a tiny side-street boutique and it caught her eye like a magnet the first time she passed. Passed, not stopping, but unable thereafter to forget the swirling pattern that wasn't really a pattern at all, but some strange sort of tie-dyed effect.

The result was an explosive mingling of pale grey and bright, vivid emerald green, an effect that shouldn't have worked, and certainly shouldn't have worked in a dress like this one. It was, by comparison to what she'd worn the evening before, almost a total antithesis. Floor length, with a high collar, full back, long sleeves and a fully-enclosed front with dozens of tiny, pearl-grey buttons.

In any other fabric, it would have been too warm for Western Australia at this time of year, but this was a light, light fabric, as Holly found when she finally worked up the nerve to go into the boutique and check—after walking past the place three times first. Even more important, it fitted her perfectly, requiring not the slightest alteration.

'It's as if it was made for you,' the sales-clerk sighed, and in her voice was truth, not any salesmanship at all.

'It was,' Holly declared. Because, to be truthful with herself, she loved the dress at first sight. The fact that it would totally forestall Wade Bannister's caressing, all-seeing eyes was also important, but secondary.

The price was right; she already had the accessories

from her grey dress, and Holly found herself leaving the shop with a new lilt to her step. Now she looked forward to attending the party, knowing that if Wade needed deep cleavages and dimpled backs to stare at, he'd have to seek elsewhere.

It didn't, unfortunately, work out quite as she expected. Wade was late, sufficiently so that Holly was dressed, ready and waiting when he rushed into the flat a few minutes before eight. He came through the door, dark hair windblown and his tie slightly askew, as if it had been open most of the day, and when he saw Holly standing nervously by the lounge room bar, glass in hand, he stopped as if he'd run into an invisible wall.

The grin that played for an instant across his mobile mouth was impossible to comprehend, difficult even to evaluate. It flickered there only an instant, joining one dark, high-raised eyebrow in a brief, unreadable message, before going again.

'Promptness is a virtue,' he muttered. 'It used to be the only one I had and now I'm entirely bereft. Forgive me, Holly. I'll only be a few minutes.'

'But ... there's no great panic,' she cried, to his departing back. Clearly Wade wasn't going to keep his lovely blonde hostess waiting, she thought as she waited patiently while he showered and changed.

When they entered the restaurant's private rooms, Holly almost wished she *had* pleaded jet-lag. Instead of the relatively small party she'd somehow anticipated, this was a full-scale, well-attended reception, and as they entered she realised that Wade knew exactly why the party was being held, and for whom.

'Happy Birthday,' he said, greeting his hostess with a bow and touching her fingers to his lips with a warm smile. 'May you have many, many more.'

'But without acknowledging them, I hope,' said

Ramona Mason. 'This is truly the last one I'll admit to for a long time to come.'

Only then did she condescend to recognise Holly, and that only briefly, with a brittle smile and icy eyes. Then she turned again to Wade.

'And thank you *so* much for the lovely present,' Ramona said in a voice like raw silk. She lifted a bejewelled hand to the fine jade necklet, leaving Holly to wonder if Wade had bought her the enormous emerald on her engagement finger or the necklet itself.

Certainly Wade himself didn't bother to enlighten Holly; he merely steered her towards the main throng of people and began a round of introductions that quickly had her head spinning with names and faces she knew she wouldn't be able to match.

Everyone, it seemed, knew Wade, but it was left to Ramona to put the cap on the introductions by announcing at one point a welcome to Australia for Holly. It was a surprising gesture of hospitality until she climaxed it by adding, 'she's Wade's housekeeper's niece from England, touring the colonies don't you know?' in tones that clearly spelled out Holly's position.

Surprisingly, nobody seemed to notice the sarcasm or the sniping, and it did not take Holly terribly long to realise that while it might have been Ramona's party, she was far from the most popular person in attendance.

Everyone was impressively pleasant to Holly, almost as if Ramona's comments had increased her popularity instead of being the put-down that was intended.

They dined on a smorgasbord that was undeniably the most magnificent piece of culinary architecture Holly had ever seen. Mountains of enormous king prawns, seas of oysters on the half-shell, islands of roast pork, beef and chicken. There were fresh fruits, literally dozens of different, delightful salads, steaming baked potatoes and cleverly decorated hillocks of potato salad.

'It looks too pretty to mess up, just to fill a few stomachs,' Holly muttered to Wade when she'd recovered from her first appraisal of the delicacies.

'The way I feel, it'll look ten times prettier once I've got a fair swack of it inside me,' he growled back. 'I've been on the go since six o'clock this morning, with only coffee for sustenance, and if you hadn't covered those succulent shoulders of yours with that dress, they'd be sporting tooth marks by now.' And his fingers traced a brief but scorching pattern across Holly's collarbone in a gesture that was so quick she couldn't be sure if it was intended to be sensuous or just to make a point of his comment.

What she did know was that it revealed the silliness of buying the dress as some sort of barrier; even through the light fabric his fingers had a magical ability to sear through to the very core of her being.

She shivered, glad that he'd turned away an instant later to reply to a question from someone beside them, and thus was unable to gauge her spontaneous reaction to his touch.

It wasn't missed, however, by their hostess. Glancing around and wondering vaguely when they'd be allowed to descend upon the smorgasbord, Holly caught Ramona's eyes on her, and the fire in them was green with unguarded emotion.

It was later in the evening, when Holly was resting between dances, that Ramona took the opportunity to speak to her in the relative privacy of the crowded room, and she made it clear immediately how she felt about Holly's presence.

'You really don't seem able to take a hint, do you?' she demanded bluntly, face smiling for the benefit of any who might see, but eyes chillingly cold.

'You probably won't believe me, but I didn't have a great deal of choice in the matter,' Holly replied calmly, trying desperately to hide the quaking within. Of all the types of confrontations she hated, this was the worst. No matter what she said, it would be wrong, yet she must somehow avoid a scene if that was what Ramona had in mind.

'I didn't notice him dragging you in kicking and screaming,' Ramona replied, and Holly couldn't hold back the giggle at this use of Wade's exact threat.

Ramona's face darkened, and Holly spoke quickly to try and placate her. 'Listen, please . . . I didn't especially want to come here tonight, but Mr Bannister did insist; he really did,' Holly said. 'And while I'm sorry if it upsets you—although I can't for the life of me imagine why it should—I'm afraid there's just nothing I can do about that. Now, if you'll excuse me . . .'

'Of course,' said the blonde, not one whit placated by Holly's attitude. 'But before you go, little missy, just a word of warning. Wade Bannister is spoken for; indeed, he's promised, if you know what I mean. I wouldn't like you to forget that.'

'I shouldn't think it's important enough—to me—to either remember or forget,' Holly replied. 'I'm here only to visit my aunt. I shan't be staying, I'm not looking for any holiday romances, or indeed any romances at all. So you can stop worrying.'

'Worrying? Why should *I* worry? The warning was just to save your dignity in case Wade decided to amuse himself during your visit, that's all.' And with that parting shot, Ramona stalked off haughtily.

It was a credible performance, Holly thought, but hardly a great one. Certainly Ramona Mason wasn't nearly as certain of Wade as she attempted to make out. That didn't really surprise Holly; who could ever be sure of a man like that, a man whose blatant, rampant sexuality lay just beneath the thin veneer of urbane calm?

Well, Ramona was certainly going to try, she thought, looking across the room to see the blonde snuggled into Wade's arms as they swirled slowly through the crowded dance floor.

'A handsome couple, aren't they?' said a voice beside her, and Holly turned to meet the eyes of Ramona's father, a tall, distinguished looking, greying man in his mid-fifties.

'Yes, they certainly are,' Holly agreed, hoping Mr Mason wasn't astute enough to read the hint of pain in her eyes at the certainty of just how handsome a couple they were.

'Still, I think we might cut an equally dashing display, don't you?' he said, leading her out on to the floor and then immediately closing her in an embrace that Holly instinctively felt inclined to repel.

Even if it had been Wade, the embrace was far too close for comfort, and as she felt the elder Mason's lips nibbling near her ear, Holly realised that he was distinctly in his cups and—worse—that he was definitely making a serious pass at her!

Oh, my God, she cried silently. In the crowded confines of the dance floor, nobody could possibly see the crude groping she was being subjected to, nor overhear the equally crude proposals to which she was expected to agree.

And there wasn't room for her to fling herself free, not that she dared make a scene, and yet she must do something!

That, providence supplied. The elder Mason stumbled, putting Holly's left knee into a position where all she need do was raise it sharply and take the questionable satisfaction of seeing his eyes blink with pain.

'Please, help me,' she cried, grabbing at the nearest masculine shoulder. 'I think he's having an attack of some sort.'

Helpful hands quickly eased the pallid figure from the dance floor, leaving Holly to make her own way to the edge of the room, where she stood trembling, hoping her stomach wouldn't choose this moment to betray her.

She stood with her head bowed, gulping in air in short, quick gasps and thanking heaven for the total coverage her gown provided. By morning, she knew, there would be black-and-blue marks in a host of places best unnoticed. Damn the man anyway, she thought, and wondered if somebody had spiked his drink or something. Based on the image he'd presented earlier in the evening, this final behaviour seemed quite out of character, but then . . .

'Are you all right?' Wade's voice cut into her thoughts like a hot knife through butter, and Holly snapped up her head with a start.

'Yes, of course,' she managed to reply, surprised and wary because of the alertness of his attitude, the harshness in his voice and eyes.

'Good, because I've made our excuses, and I think we'd best leave. Now.'

'I . . . all right,' she agreed. Lord, how could he be so angry? He couldn't possibly see what she'd done, or had he, by some miraculous mischance?

He stood beside her in the lift like some living, deep-breathing statue, silent and yet projecting an aura of anger that was tangible in the crowded lift. Only when they were in the privacy of the flat did he speak, and then his voice was ragged with scarce-subdued anger.

'All right. I know what you did. Now I want to know why, and I warn you, it had better be good!'

CHAPTER THREE

'I SHOULD think the answer would be obvious; I was quite seriously provoked,' Holly replied, forcing herself to meet those icy green eyes.

'By Alan Mason? You've got to be joking.'

'I assure you that I am not joking, even though I find the truth as difficult to accept as you must—and I was there,' Holly cried. 'But the fact is that he was all over me like a rash. I . . . I think he must have had too much to drink.'

'And you, of course, did absolutely nothing to provoke this, this assault?' It wasn't really a question; he was thinking out loud, Holly thought, but that didn't stop her passionate denial.

'I most certainly did not. I was standing there, alone, and he asked me to dance, which certainly didn't seem unreasonable. But we no sooner got out on the floor than he . . . well . . . he became quite unmanageable.'

'*That* unmanageable? Bloody hell, Holly, you damned near ruined him for life.'

'I know, and believe me when I say that I'm sorry about it,' Holly replied, trembling now. She hadn't meant to seriously injure the man, merely to allay his intentions in a fashion that would get her free of the situation.

'But what else could I do, short of creating a tremendous scene? At least this way everybody thinks he had an attack of some kind, which is surely better than . . .'

'Everybody who didn't see as clearly as I did,' Wade interrupted. 'Which, for your sake, I hope was indeed

everybody. But ... Alan Mason? I don't deny that he
might have been attracted to you; he as much as told
me so. But to have warranted such a response ... I
can't believe that.'

'Well if you'd like to hold off your high-and-mighty
judgment until morning, I'll show you the bruises,'
Holly snapped, her own temper now raging to match
his disbelief.

'I don't know why, and I don't care why. For all I
know his loving daughter put him up to it, but the fact
is that nobody is going to manhandle me like that and
expect me to put up with it. Nobody. It was ... it was
just disgusting.'

Whereupon her nerve broke, and Holly fled to her
room in total disarray, only vaguely aware as she
slammed the door that the front door of the flat was
also being closed rather violently, with Wade Bannister
on the outside.

She cried briefly, then undressed and threw herself
into the shower, scouring away the memory of Alan
Mason's assault and wishing she could also wash away
her remembrance of his verbal approach, which had
been even worse.

An hour later, with no indication that Wade had or
would return, she slipped into bed and after another
hour of restlessness, was asleep. Once there, she slept
well, waking refreshed and feeling much more able to
cope with Wade's accusations, but surprisingly, there
was no need of that.

When Holly had done her ablutions and put on her
gown to go out into the sitting room, breakfast was just
arriving and Wade Bannister was there waiting for it.

'Good morning,' he said, cheerful and smiling as if
they'd parted the night before on the most amicable of
terms.

Holly smiled in return, but inwardly she was

frowning at the questions that kept forming in her wariness. Why was he being so pleasant? What was he scheming about?

Had he just arrived, she found herself wondering, after spending the night consoling Ramona Mason? Certainly he'd got back early enough to have changed; his casual denim trousers and shirt, open halfway to the waist and with the sleeves rolled up along bronzed, muscular arms, presented a distinct change from the immaculate evening attire in which she'd last seen him.

Holly watched as breakfast was laid, then closed her eyes in sober thought. She hadn't, she suddenly realised, even bothered to lock the door to her room. Nor had she bothered to sleep covered up, it being unseasonably warm. What if he had . . . ?

She looked up, unable to halt the slight flush that rose from the neckline of the robe. And, as she might have expected, he was not only watching, but apparently reading her mind as well.

'Stop trying to appear modest,' he grinned. 'And don't bother to ask if I looked in on you during the night or even came in to tuck you in, because I wouldn't tell you if you did. Although, considering the effectiveness of your defences, I'm not all that sure anybody but a damned fool would have dared.'

He was laughing at her, Holly decided, though his voice was no more than a warm, gentle chuckle. And he *had* looked in to check on her; what's more, he didn't really care that she knew it.

'I'm sure you had other things to keep you occupied; I only hope you enjoyed yourself,' she replied in tones as level as she could keep them. 'When did you get back, or am I not allowed to ask?'

He shrugged. 'While you were sleeping, obviously. I didn't bother to write down the exact time or anything. Why—would it matter?'

'Certainly not to me,' she replied. 'But it obviously wasn't early, because I lay awake for quite awhile and didn't hear you come in.'

'Maybe you slept earlier and more soundly than you think,' he replied, devilish lights hovering behind those clear green eyes. Wade Bannister certainly didn't appear to be suffering the ravages of a late night.

'Probably because I've got a clear conscience,' Holly retorted, thoroughly convinced now that he was laughing at her, mocking her. And not pleased at either prospect. 'And you might also have *asked* what I wanted for breakfast, instead of being your usual arrogant self.'

'Oh, sit down and eat,' Wade replied, this time with a distinctly weary shake of his head. 'It's obvious a good night's sleep didn't do much for your disposition; maybe a decent breakfast will at least make you fit to associate with.'

'I wouldn't count on that,' Holly replied. But she did obey the directive, listening with dismay as her stomach registered unexpected approval of the cereal, steak-and-eggs, toast and coffee, with a resounding growl.

'Nice to see some sign of appreciation,' he remarked dryly, then laughed at her obvious embarrassment. 'Oh, for God's sake, Holly, stop trying to be such a pain. I'm sure that with the same amount of effort, and probably a lot less, you could actually be a fairly likeable person if you tried.'

'And how absolutely observant of you to have noticed,' she replied in a voice that dripped acid. 'Would you please pass the sugar before my coffee gets any cooler.'

Such requests were about the extent of the conversation until the meal was over. Holly was in no mood to be sociable, and Wade, for whatever reasons, didn't push her any more.

Not, at least, until he was able to light a cigarette, lean back comfortably in his chair, and let his eyes roam significantly over the array of dishes, bowls and cups—all of them empty.

'Well, my choice couldn't have been that bad,' he observed, though not speaking directly to Holly. He chose instead to direct his remarks to an invisible, non-existent third person, accompanying the comments with expansive gestures.

'Of course, left to her own devices, she'd have chosen tea and toast, or some such thing, been too proud to admit that it was an insufficient breakfast for a growing girl, and then suffered tremendous agony until she got into the airplane and could stock up on the bitsy little plastic sandwich things they call food in the sky. Very tough on the disposition; her aunt would have had my guts for garters when the poor child staggered off the plane in the last throes of sheer starvation . . .'

'Oh . . . stop it,' Holly cried, unable to withstand the urge to laugh at his absurd histrionics.

'Good,' he said with exaggerated smugness. 'I'm glad to see that you've got a sense of humour, at least.'

Holly was less surprised that *he* had, but held her tongue on that subject. He was probably, she thought, just a bit light-headed after having had very little sleep. Except that he looked remarkably well rested for a man who . . . no! She mustn't think about that. It was, she decided, very much none of her business. Why shouldn't he spend his last night in Perth with Ramona Mason? Certainly the blonde had made her own wishes on that subject clear enough, Holly's presence notwithstanding.

And she had to control an involuntary flush as she glanced over to see Wade watching her, obviously in tune to her thinking. But he didn't bother to jibe her about it.

'Are you sure you got enough to eat? If not, you'd better say so now, because we're running short of time,' he said. And she couldn't quite tell if he was having a go at her or not.

'I've had quite sufficient, thank you,' she replied, certain she wouldn't have to eat again that day, not after such an enormous breakfast.

'Right, then go get yourself together. I wouldn't want you to miss your plane.'

The implication was too obvious, too tempting a lure to be resisted even on a full stomach. '*My* plane?' Holly asked almost before she thought. Surely he was leading her on. After all his insistence that she wait so they could fly north together, and now he wasn't coming?

'Your plane,' he confirmed. 'I'll drive you to the airport and see you off, but I won't be coming with you. I've discovered some ... business that I have to take care of here.'

Business? Holly could just imagine what kind of business. Tall and blonde and nearly certain of Wade Bannister. Did he realise, she wondered? Or was he so sure of himself, secure in his intense masculinity, that Ramona Mason's certainty didn't particularly worry him?

'I'm surprised you think I can be trusted alone,' she said, being deliberately bitchy and both loving the sensation and hating herself for doing it.

He only shrugged. 'Don't let's start that again. It's over.'

'Not that it matters anyway.' The words were out before she thought, but they didn't sound regretful. Only bitchy.

Suddenly Wade was on his feet, looming over her with a quite distracting proximity. Holly couldn't help but think of the power in those huge hands, the sheer physical presence that seemed to radiate from him like heat from a furnace.

'No,' he said, voice strangely soft. 'No, it doesn't seem to matter, does it? Tell me, dear Miss Grange ... what is it with you? First you are all shirty because you couldn't have your own way; now you've got it and you're still being hard to get on with. Are you always so difficult, or is it just me that makes you that way?'

'I'm not at all hard to get along with,' Holly retorted, not at all comfortable, either, at having to crane her neck to meet his eyes. Standing over her like that seemed to just increase his power, to make her increasingly vulnerable. Especially, she realised, since his position gave him an unrestricted view down the half-open front of her gown.

And again, as if he was reading her mind, Wade grinned as she hastily reached to pull the gown closer around her throat and breasts.

'Modesty? So soon after breakfast? Oh, spare me that, please. Besides, it's nothing I haven't seen before. In fact, it isn't half so provocative as that dress you wore last night; I'm not surprised poor old Alan Mason blotted his copy book—you've no idea how close I came to it myself.'

'Damn you!' Holly cried, thrusting out of her chair to stand before him, her eyes snapping with frustration as she trembled in her need to strike out at him.

It was no contest. He stood there, hands on his hips as he quite deliberately surveyed her face and figure with bold, if not hungry eyes. 'I really do wish you'd clean up your language,' he said. 'What's your aunt going to think if you go swearing like that every time my name's mentioned?'

'Obviously she doesn't know you as I do, or she'd very likely do some swearing of her own,' Holly retorted. 'I really don't know how she can stand to work for anyone as chauvinistic and arrogant as you are.'

'Well then you'll just have to ask her, won't you?' he chuckled. 'Who knows, you just might learn something.'

'About you? I already know more than I want to,' she sneered back. 'And none of it, I assure you, is very much worth the trouble involved.'

'Oh? Funny, I'd have thought differently,' he drawled, reaching out to take her gently by the shoulders. His hands seemed to move in slow motion, but Holly's body was even slower. She moved away, her mind solid in its resistance, but it was as if she were nailed to the floor, unable to shift quickly enough to evade his touch.

She was powerless once his fingers closed on her upper arms, drawing her softly to him as his mouth dipped to capture her lips. His eyes locked on hers, holding her, compelling her to keep looking up, to disobey the mind that screamed at her to turn away from his kiss, to struggle free, to fight.

'I wonder if all this bad temper is the result of me not joining you last night,' he mused in a husky voice just before his lips closed on Holly's mouth, ignoring her futile struggles as he kissed with experienced, deliberate thoroughness.

She could feel the male hardness of him through the thin gown as his arms slid lower to clasp her against him, and despite her mental rejection, Holly knew only too quickly that her body didn't, couldn't, share that rejection. As her lips moulded to follow the path of his mouth on hers, she knew she should be screaming her objections, but her mouth only wanted more of him.

The arms that raised to flail at him, to claw her way to freedom, instead ended up curved across his shoulders, her fingers unable to do more than tangle themselves in the hair at his nape, helping to hold them together in an embrace that grew increasingly passionate as Holly's mental resistance also faded before the insistent clamour of her heart.

It was madness! But such madness she'd never experienced, never even dreamed of. When he freed her long enough for his roving hand to seek the opening of her gown, she twisted not in flight, but to ease his access, revelling in his touch.

And the touch of his fingers on her breasts was like the gentle caress of a sunbeam, at first. Only when her body cried out in silent response did his caress become more and more insistent, stroking and lifting her responses until she thought she could take no more, until she thought she would swoon at the sheer ecstasy of it.

The gown had fallen open, allowing his hands access, and now he maneouvred her so that his mouth, too, could reach, gliding like quicksilver down the hollow of her throat, his tongue in the hollow between her breasts.

Holly reeled as the waves of sensation flowed through her, her hands clasping at his broad shoulders for the support she must have, lest she fall. Then his hands were firm at her waist, steadying her before one hand freed itself to begin a journey across her hips, across the flatness of her stomach and thence to the centre of her universe, lifting her into a riotous sunburst of sensation.

Holly was crying out; she could hear her voice, if not distinguish the words, yet she knew they were not cries of objection. She wanted him as she had never wanted anything, wanted him to possess her, to conquer her, to continue his lovemaking to its ultimate, inevitable conclusion, to bring her the fulfilment she now craved with addictive necessity.

Her body had abandoned all reason; her mind was drugged by the intensity of her own responses. As his mouth lifted from her breasts, cruising trails of sensation back up to where her lips waited impatiently, her own hands searched across the furry expanse of his chest, then lower to unbutton the rest of his shirt and explore the muscular body thus revealed. She felt his belt buckle beneath her fingers, then sent them lower, seeking the essence of maleness her body so avidly craved.

Wade groaned at her touch, the groan mingling with the sweetness of his breath in her mouth, mingling with the roar of her own feminine aliveness at his touch on her body.

Then he was lifting her, the untied robe flowing behind as he carried her in his arms, locking her spirit to him with his lips as they moved across the room, holding her as he fumbled only an instant in opening the door to his bedroom.

He placed her on the bed gently, holding her without force as he shed his shirt with one hand, then reached to undo his belt, allowing his trousers to slip to the floor.

Holly's voice was a soughing murmur of acceptance, even of encouragement, but the strident demand of the telephone made Wade's response an evocative curse as he saw and felt the sound haul her back to the borders of reality. Not all the way, but far enough that her conscience cried out in alarm at the nearness of her total surrender.

And yet, she cried out as he left her, cried in a silent scream from the very core of her existence, a scream that denied the logic, the orders of her conscious mind. Her mind sought sanctuary even as he slipped from the room, but her body was vapid, listless, lolling in the fleeing memories of new and wonderful sensation. She heard his voice, ragged and uneven, as he answered the telephone. Heard him say with quite undisguised frustration, 'Damn it, Ramona, but you've got a deplorable sense of timing.'

And she heard him say something about being pulled
from the shower, but that, she heard over her shoulder
as she fled, spurred into movement by the blonde
woman's name as if she'd been struck by a stockwhip.

Moments later and she was reeling with shock as her
body was ravaged by the icy blast of her shower, and
Holly sucked in her breath and refused to reach out for
the moderating hot tap, choosing instead the punishment that would perhaps erase the longing, wipe away
the memory of ecstasy, wash off the scent and the taste
and the feel of *him*.

She stayed in the shower, secure in the chill and the
knowledge that the door between them was locked; she
was safe. Until she heard a knock and his voice: 'You'd
better hurry now, unless you want to miss your flight.'

No sign of ragged passion in the voice now. Even
above the roar of the shower it registered a calm, an
acceptance. The moment, for what it had been worth,
was over. And maybe, she thought, he would even
forget it. But would she?

Holly hurried through the process of dressing and
packing, hurried with a body that seemed only half to
belong to her and only half able to function. She
walked as if knee-deep in water, unable to create or
maintain momentum from legs that so recently had
trembled with the rising passion of Wade's touch.

But at least, she thought with some semblance of
relief, luck—or Ramona's good management—or both,
had caused that timely phone call. Without it, her
response to Wade Bannister would have been so
complete, so abandoned, so wanton, that any respect he
might have for her would have gone like thistledown in
the wind.

And she wanted him to respect her, to believe in her.
Wanted it more than anything else in the world—
excepting perhaps the man himself. But had their

lovemaking been consummated, here, this morning, on his bed, it would have been with such enthusiasm on her part that he couldn't possibly ever believe her to be the inexperienced lover she was.

Looking at herself during a final check in the bathroom mirror, Holly saw wide, bright eyes, eyes alive now with the knowledge—the hellish knowledge—that she was falling in love with a man who had reason to believe her a wanton, and whose effect upon her physically was just that—but for him alone. Only how could she expect him to believe that?

It simply wasn't fair. The effect of his eavesdropping at the airport, the untruth of it so unprovable, seemed to loom like a spectre over their entire relationship. She couldn't, Holly thought, have competed successfully against someone with Ramona Mason's experience at the best of times, but with this singular handicap she had no chance at all.

But probably she wouldn't have stood a chance anyway, Holly thought as she emerged from the bedroom to meet Wade's impatient glance. Even if he hadn't thought she was the kind of girl she wasn't. Holly simply didn't have the kind of cool sophistication and poise that Ramona possessed, could never provide the type of social function to a marriage that Ramona could.

Wade, thankfully, said virtually nothing during their drive to the airport. Holly didn't know what she might have done if he'd decided to discuss what the phone call had so shockingly interrupted. She didn't, somewhat to her own surprise, feel any great guilt about it. But she certainly didn't want to talk about it! And, she realised, if there had only been some indication that Wade's feelings matched the ones she knew were growing within her, there'd have been no guilt at all except for having been stopped.

As it was, she regretted having allowed her body to betray her into giving herself to him without a word of love, without even the remote suggestion of it. Certainly not from him, she thought, watching sideways to see what might be revealed by his expression.

Nothing! Their interlude was over and Holly reached the airport convinced she had returned to being nothing but a problem to the man she knew she loved beyond redemption.

Upon their arrival at the airport, he assisted in checking her luggage, saw her to the appropriate departure lounge, but made no attempt to lighten her mood with idle conversation. It was as if the morning's lovemaking hadn't even happened, there wasn't a hint of apology in his voice or attitude, probably, Holly thought, because he wasn't the slightest bit sorry for anything but having been interrupted.

Did she even want an apology? Not really; she didn't want any man—especially Wade—to feel sorry for having tried to make love to her.

But his silence bothered her slightly, along with the way he kept looking at her when he thought she mightn't notice. They weren't sly or cunning glances, but introspective, as if he might be—finally—reassessing her. Yet that, Holly decided, was most unlikely.

It was also distressing and annoying, especially when he only touched her forehead with his lips in farewell, although his voice was gentle. 'You have a good flight,' he smiled, 'and tell Jessica I'll see you both in two or three days. Four at the very most.'

Damn the man! Did he not realise what he was doing to her? Or did he realise it only too well, she wondered?

The flight north wasn't really the one Holly might have chosen for herself. It was the 'milk run' that stopped briefly in a series of strangely named little communities, all of them much of a muchness since she saw only their airports and the countryside as the aircraft took off and landed. It was a landscape that grew increasingly drier and more barren looking, a wild, untamed landscape that seemed scarcely fit for humans.

'From some points of view, it's like the backside of the moon,' Wade had said during one of their discussions. She had to agree.

And from the names on the airline magazine's route map, it might well have been the moon, especially for somebody fresh from England and unused to the unique Australianisms.

Holly's route included Geraldton, Carnarvon, Learmonth and Karratha, but a different choice of flights could have shown her airports at Tom Price or Newman or—and she quite regretted missing this one—Paraburdoo. There was little to choose from between the smaller of the airports, but the passengers were a living kaleidoscope in themselves.

Asians, Blacks, Europeans and dinkum Australians were mingled in a situation far less formal than the seating of her international flight. Oil workers, many of them American, spent the entire journey guzzling tins of beer as if they'd die of thirst without it.

There was certainly no shortage of money, judging from a poker game that kept half-a-dozen workers busy, and everyone on the aircraft bar one or two Aboriginals was expensively if casually dressed. Some of the Asians, in particular, seemed veritable peacocks in their over-bright, flamboyant clothing, although their voices were liquid and soft.

It came as something of a surprise when the captain announced on their arrival to Port Hedland that the ground temperature was forty-four degrees. A hundred and ten on the fahrenheit scale! Even mention of such

temperatures in Jessica's letters hadn't prepared Holly
for the blandness with which the simple announcement
was made. At each of the preceding stops, the outdoor
temperature had seemed warm, but not severe enough
to be upsetting on the short dash from air-conditioned
plane to air-conditioned terminal.

Of course Jessica's—Wade's—house was also air-
conditioned, Holly realised, but how on earth did
people survive such incredible temperatures out in the
open?

As the aircraft began its circling approach she looked
out of the tiny window and was surprised again. There
was nothing, or almost nothing, to see. Only vast
expanses of reddish, ochre-tinged ground. And then
enormous, obviously man-made layouts of dazzling
whiteness. Salt pans? And finally she saw what
appeared to be a settlement, nearly lost in the heat-haze
and camouflaged by the coating of dust that seemed to
make every roof the same colour as the landscape. Only
the blue-green waters of the adjoining sea provided any
contrast.

And then they were down, taxiing up to a low,
spreading terminal building that sat almost alone in the
forbidding emptiness. Vaguely human shapes could be
seen behind glass doors, but apart from the essential
airport crew, there was no one waiting outside for the
aircraft to come to a halt.

Once outside, Holly realised why. It was like walking
into some enormous furnace. There was a breeze, but it
was hot! No cooling effect, but she could feel the
perspiration lifted from her skin as if by a sponge. Like
everyone else, she made the journey to the terminal at a
half-trot, her body instinctively seeking the shade of the
entry-way.

Would Wade have moved thus, she wondered, or
would he be immune to the intense heat, strolling along

in his larger-than-life strides without even noticing it. A hundred and ten! She felt desiccated, like a dried-up prune, by the time she reached the terminal. But inside it was cool, and busy, alive with people coming and going, meeting friends and relatives with loud cries in myriad languages, children everywhere.

And Aunt Jessica!

Even Wade Bannister was forgotten momentarily in the joy of seeing her diminutive aunt again. The tiny, bird-like woman still looked as she had when Holly had last seen her, years and years, almost a lifetime before.

Tidy, spry, and so quick-moving she seemed always to be sprinting, she flung herself forward to wrap unexpectedly strong arms around Holly and clasp her tightly.

Both had tears in their eyes when the embrace was over, but they were joyful tears, freely shed. 'You look marvellous,' Jessica said. 'Even better than your pictures.'

'And so do you,' Holly replied. But she was lying. Because Jessica didn't really look well at all, not up close.

Beneath the deep, tropical tan, her face was pale with the pallidness of strain, and her lips held a slightly blueish caste. The hair that Holly remembered as a shining black cap now looked as if Jessica had been standing in a snowstorm, and there were lines of suffering in her face beyond her years.

Only the eyes remained unchanged from memory; black, snapping eyes that observed the world through lenses of both compassion and cynicism. Darker, older versions of Holly's own grey eyes.

They headed for 'home' once Holly's luggage was unloaded, driving in a large, air-conditioned station sedan. Wade's, of course. The route led straight into the flat vastness of the Northwest scrub country, where

spinifex and saltbush did an apparently inefficient job
of covering the red-yellow soil and there wasn't a hill to
be seen. Past a huge elevator that stockpiled salt like a
mountain of snow, incongruous in the blistering heat,
past a turnoff that Jessica said went to the dormitory
community of South Hedland.

'And iron ore is the reason for just about all of it,'
Jessica explained as they drove on towards Port Hedland
itself. 'There were only about twelve hundred people
here in 1965, when the development programme started.
Now there would be more than ten times that many,
and the place is still growing. South Hedland was built
because Port Hedland is really located on an island, and
they simply ran out of building space. Of course, with
road and rail construction it isn't an island anymore,
but that didn't change the space limitations.

'But Finucane Island—that's the headquarters for
Goldsworthy Mining—is still really an island as far as
we're concerned here,' she continued. 'Oh, there's a
road to it, and the railway, of course. But the place is
twenty-seven kilometres away by road, despite being
just over there across the harbour.'

She volunteered to give Holly the 'two-bob' tour, and
after pointing to where they would normally have
turned off for 'home', carried on along a bitumen road
that was paralleled by a railroad on their left.

Ahead was a veritable mountain of red-grey material
that seemed to go on forever beside the railway track,
and Jessica waved casually at it. 'Iron ore stockpile—
Mountain Newman Mining,' she said. 'That's what all
this is about—everything! If it wasn't for the iron ore, I
think the whole town might close down, although that's
certainly not fair to say, since the town was here long
before the mining companies.'

The downtown area, such as it was, seemed
overshadowed by the mountainous iron-ore stockpile

and the vastness of the port facilities that seemed to grow right out of the main street.

The town was almost a hundred years old, Holly was told, and yet even the older sections had a rawness, a sense of newness despite the overall blanket of ore dust. There seemed to be no sense of plan; a few shops on one street, a few more on the next, with vacant allotments or elderly houses scattered between. Not, Holly decided, very much of a town at all. She wondered if South Hedland, being so much newer, was much different.

'Oh, it's that much more modern, of course,' Jessica said. 'And it's got a big, air-conditioned shopping centre and a tavern, and most of the government offices and such. I expect that eventually *this* will become the satellite town in reality, but not quite yet.'

Holly noticed that her aunt seemed preoccupied, and though she was free enough with trivial tourist information, it was clear she had other, presumably more important things on her mind. When Holly suggested they postpone the rest of the tour, Jessica hastily agreed, appearing somewhat relieved to do so.

The house owned by Wade Bannister wasn't outwardly that much more impressive than any of the others in the subdivision of Cooke Point, but the established gardens gave it a vaguely more permanent look. It was large and low, constructed of dark brick, and so cool inside because of the ducted air-conditioning that Holly found herself shivering slightly.

Jessica threw a blistering look at the thermostat and said, 'Perhaps I'd best turn that thing down. We hardly ever use it, as a general rule, except on really hot days like this. I don't mind the heat, and of course Wade is so much out-of-doors that he feels he must stay used to it regardless.'

It was, Holly realised with surprise, the first time

Wade's name had been mentioned, and for whatever reason, she felt a cold shiver of a quite different type slither down her spine.

She had only the briefest of respites while Jessica poured them both a tall glass of lemonade; then the expected inquisition began in earnest.

'You didn't like Wade.' It was neither question, not entirely a statement all on its own. Jessica hadn't reached her time of life as a world traveller without considerable intuition.

'We ... could have got along better, I suppose,' Holly replied carefully. 'But I wouldn't go so far as to say that I didn't, don't like him. He's just a ... very dominant type.'

'What everybody calls a man's man,' Jessica retorted. 'Just a pity so few people recognise that a woman's man is usually just exactly the same. What happened—did he make love to you?'

Holly gasped at the uncanny accuracy of the question, then covered up as best she could by faking a sneeze. Probably in vain, but she wasn't at all prepared for such direct and accurate questioning.

'It was more of a personality clash than anything,' Holly replied, choosing her words carefully. 'We weren't together long enough to, well, to get all that close.'

'Rubbish!' Jessica belied her ageing spinster status with a broad-mindedness that most girls Holly's age might have envied, although Holly didn't, especially not right now. 'You spent, by my count, something like two days and two nights together; that's more than enough time.'

Holly was astonished at Jessica's candour, but determined not to allow the discussion to proceed much longer without some definite clarifications.

'Most of that time, I was alseep,' she countered. 'And

we certainly didn't spend last night together; I think that pleasure belongs to one Ramona Mason, who's very lovely, blonde . . .'

'And a first rate pain in the . . . neck,' Jessica snorted. 'The only reason I could see for Wade spending the night with her is if the air-conditioner broke down. Especially after seeing you. You're lovelier than any of your pictures, Holly.'

'Which means nothing at all and you know it,' Holly laughed. 'I'm sure Ramona Mason is much more his type, and personally I wish her well of him.'

Jessica regarded her soberly. 'My, my,' she said. 'You two really didn't hit it off well at all, did you? Which is quite probably all my fault. I have to admit that I did rather . . .'

'It's called matchmaking,' Holly interrupted in her most severe voice. 'And yes, I rather think you did. Which,' she added, 'pleaseth me not at all.'

Then she laughed, hoping to ease the look of strain that flowed like a shadow across Jessica's face. 'But don't worry about it. I'm sure your Mr Bannister and I can get along well enough to last my visit.'

And she laughed again. 'Besides, you've said in your letters he's hardly ever here, and it's you I've come to see, anyway.'

'Yes, well.' And the worried look was more than a shadow now. 'Did he say when he'd be back, specifically?'

'Just in a day or two or three. Four at the most. But why?'

'Because I'm not going to be here,' Jessica said, shaking her head as the significance of the remark became evident on Holly's startled face. 'I must fly to Perth, you see. Tomorrow!'

CHAPTER FOUR

HOLLY was stunned!

'Tomorrow. But ... but ...' She stammered in her confusion. Further words were captured on her tongue as if it were glue.

'Yes, tomorrow. Oh, Holly, I wouldn't, didn't intend to leave you alone. I didn't even intend you to know about my tests. Or Wade. Until this cropped up. I just got word from my own doctor this morning. No, it isn't really serious,' she added, 'so stop looking at me like that. It's bad enough Wade fussing over me all the time without you doing it too.'

'Well it certainly must be fairly serious if you have to go all the way to Perth for tests,' Holly exclaimed.

'I tell you it *isn't* serious,' Jessica insisted. 'Just a few tests that can't be done here. The serious part is the timing. I feel horrible about having to leave you here alone so soon after you've arrived.'

'Yes, the timing certainly isn't the best,' Holly agreed. 'But only because if we'd known, if you'd told Wade ... Mr Bannister when he phoned, then I could have stayed in Perth and been company for you.'

'Oh, no,' Holly's aunt proclaimed in tones that revealed she'd already thought of that. 'One of us would have to be here, you see, to look after the house. You don't leave houses sitting vacant in Port Hedland, not even for a few days. Not in cyclone season.'

'Not in any season, I should imagine,' Holly said. 'Judging from the security measures, it must be a terrible place to live.'

She was somewhat taken aback by Jessica's immediate

laughter, and not entirely without reason. One of the first things she'd noticed about Port Hedland was how every home had massive security screens at every window. And here inside Wade's house, the exit doors all had four separate bolts on the inside. It was like an armed fortress!

Jessica followed Holly's gaze, then laughed again as she rose, gesturing to Holly to follow. They entered the house's main bathroom, and it, too, had the required heavy bolts.

'The security isn't from people; it's in case of cyclones,' Jessica explained. 'The greatest danger in a cyclone is from the things being blown about by the winds—which can reach two hundred kilometers an hour. Anything left lying around—and I mean *anything*—becomes a deadly missile under those circumstances. And in a really bad cyclone, the house itself could come apart, which is why the bathroom is designed to be a sort of shelter.'

Holly shuddered. 'It's difficult to imagine,' she said.

'Not when you've lived through one. I was here for Dean, which was only a baby when compared to Tracy, which destroyed Darwin on Christmas morning back in 1974. Dean was as bad as I ever want to see, thank you very much!'

'Yes, I remember reading about Darwin, and seeing the television reports,' Holly said. 'But surely, that was unusual? I mean, all cyclones can't be that bad?'

'Every one has the same potential,' Jessica replied soberly. 'It's more good luck than anything else that some are much less destructive than others. With any luck at all, you won't even get to hear of a cyclone while you're here, but by the same token, we could have one start up tomorrow. So I want you to read all the literature on what to do; it's more important than you'd realise, never having been through a cyclone.'

She spent the next half hour showing Holly the steps to be taken, explaining the cyclone warning system and the rules that accompanied it, and also explaining in more detail the aspects of her own role in Wade's home.

Most proper house-sitters, she explained, were locals who lived in caravans or temporary accommodation except when called in to care for a house when the owners were absent, usually in a situation of long-service leave or holidays.

'I'm in a different situation,' she explained, 'because Wade is on the move so much. I'm actually a combination of conventional housekeeper and house-sitter, as he's so often called out on very short notice.'

Part of Wade's house was designed as a 'granny flat', a self-contained unit in which a housekeeper, children's help or relative could live with reasonable privacy while still being conveniently close to the family.

'In my case, the flat is something of a waste,' Jessica said, 'because Wade insists on treating me more like a mother than a housekeeper, even when he's home. But you might find the privacy comforting; the Northwest has a casual attitude that even southerners find a bit trying at times.'

Despite the outlandish temperatures outside, the two women ate a light but filling dinner, then spent the evening chatting before making an early night of it. Holly began to relax, very comfortable in Jessica's company despite unspoken fears at the reception she might expect when the time came to share the house with only Wade Bannister himself.

She had a room to herself in the flat, and no fears about occupying herself in Jessica's absence, but dealing with Wade, she thought, might be a problem.

'I'd almost rather face a cyclone,' she mused half-aloud, once secure in her room. Jessica's astute understanding of the situation didn't help either, but it was her own vulnerability that worried Holly the most. How could she maintain any impression of respectability when all Wade had to do was touch her and she collapsed in a heap of wanton sexuality?

But at the very least, she thought, I can manage not to aggravate the situation. Whether we get along is less important than Jessica's health, and even Wade can't argue against that.

Holly drove Jessica to the airport next morning, and was far too concerned afterwards with finding her way home again than worrying about Wade Bannister. With any luck, he'd stay over in Perth until the tests were completed, which Jessica insisted would take only three days at most.

And what if he did return first? At least in this large house they could manage to stay out of one another's way, Holly thought. It would definitely be a less explosive scene than that damned flat.

What bothered her the most was Jessica's eventual admission that the matchmaking was no spur-of-the-moment thing, but had actually been a lengthy campaign that had merely intensified with Holly's decision to visit her. She had shown Wade Holly's pictures, read him her letters, done everything but organise the two of them as pen-friends. Hardly any wonder he'd been outraged at her giving him first impressions that she was no better than a gold-digger, and even less likely now that he'd ever totally forget that first meeting.

Holly spent most of the day driving around Port Hedland, eyes wide with wonder at the bustle and activity. Even in the heat of the day, she found men working shirtless and hatless out-of-doors, women shopping with small children, roads filled with traffic.

It was a strange, unnerving sort of heat, Holly found. The air was so dry she could almost feel it plucking the

moisture from her skin, and despite the car radio's
assurance that it was thirty-nine degrees, far hotter than
anything she'd ever experienced in Britain, simply
stepping into the shade produced astonishing cooling
effects.

But it was still too warm to consider a hot meal that
evening, even if she could have bothered cooking just
for herself. Some cold meat and salad sufficed
admirably, and she was asleep by nine o'clock after a
half-hearted attempt to watch the town's single
television channel.

She was up with the sun, next morning, determined
to take advantage of the early hours' relative coolness
to potter in the garden and get a start on her suntan at
the same time. Wearing only a pale turquoise bikini and
some borrowed gardening gloves, she spent a pleasant
hour weeding the flower beds, shifting from sun to
shade in a regular pattern and acutely conscious of the
dangers of sunstroke in such a climate.

It was the garden of Wade's house, she decided, that
declared the nature of the owner. There was a judicious
mixture of orderliness and nature taking its own course,
but the overall effect was of a property well cared for,
appreciated. So many of the homes she'd seen in Port
Hedland, especially in the newer suburbs, seemed raw,
ill-kept and somehow impermanent.

Jessica had explained the reasons. Port Hedland,
she'd said, was to all intents and purposes a company
town. Despite having existed as a community for nearly
a century, the town as it now stood was almost entirely
the entity of the mining firms, and company employees
were catered for in the extreme.

'Their rents are subsidised, they've got an excellent
home purchase scheme, paid holidays like you wouldn't
believe. The company does just about everything for
them,' she'd said. 'At one time—I believe it's now

changed—the company would send an electrician all the way out to South Hedland just to change a lightbulb or replace a fuse. True! And what's worse, a fair proportion of employees would think such a service was normal! Spoiled rotten, I say, but that's the way of it. The company established most of the social facilities in the town, built most of the houses, did just about everything. And gets damned little credit for it, although I do feel there's probably fair value given somewhere along the line. But you'd know from your sociology studies, Holly, that the more people are given, the more they want—and the less they'll do for themselves. That's why so many of the homes are in a mess; people just take the attitude that the company should do everything.'

There were also, Jessica had said, a variety of special concessions to all people employed in the development of the country's northern, isolated regions. Special tax concessions applied to workers 'north of the 26th' although not even Jess could explain what bureaucrat had selected that particular line of latitude to establish northern concessions. Or why.

The reasons were manifold and made some sense. Tremendous distances were involved. Perth was nearly three thousand kilometres from Adelaide, the nearest of the 'eastern' cities, and that distance was mostly through the vastness of the Nullarbor Plain. Port Hedland was yet another two thousand kilometres to the north of Perth, and such distances created vivid price distinctions and an undeniable isolation factor. The concessions were required to stimulate development by making it attractive to workers, giving them a bit of a push to move north and stay.

But it wasn't a complete success. The kaleidoscope of heat, drought, the 'wet' of the monsoon season, the cyclone risks and the sheer isolation all combined to take a toll of the work force. There was a tremendous turnover in Port Hedland's population, Jessica said, with a three-year stay about average.

'It's the kind of country you either love or you hate,' she'd said. 'Personally, I love it, but most people come north for the money and when they've made their stake they get out as fast as they can. And because it's such a *new* town, in so many ways, the social order isn't the same. There are very few grandparents, for instance, very few people with actual roots.'

Wiping away a trickle of perspiration, Holly wondered if *she* could ever put down roots in such a place. Or were her roots already planted, in Britain?

Certainly it appeared that Wade Bannister was a Northwester to the core. Jessica had said he'd actually been born in Port Hedland, although of course he'd gone south to Perth for his education and then overseas to get even more experience as a geologist and mining engineer.

The shade of the patio, where a hammock was slung between two of the uprights, finally claimed Holly's attention. She sprawled into the resilient netting, surprised at how quick the heat and sun had sapped her strength, but quite sure she'd been properly careful not to get too much sun. Setting the hammock in motion, she closed her eyes against the glare and relaxed into daydreams that as quickly became ordinary dreams. The nightmare started when she woke up!

'Is this some new luncheon dish you're planning— broiled Hollyhock?' And there was no mistaking the voice that shattered her nap, nor the bite of sarcasm in it.

Holly opened her eyes to find Wade Bannister, hands on his hips as he shook his head from side to side, his lips quirked in a half-amused grin.

She didn't understand his question until she started

to get up and found the world swinging dizzily around her. By then it was too late; Wade was already leaning down to scoop her into his arms, muttering something beneath his breath that she was just as glad not to hear.

'Put me down!' she started to cry, but then the pain began, a ringing shrieking pain that started between her eyes and seemed to lash like a stockwhip inside her head.

And with it the realisation of tenderness. Wade couldn't have lifted her more gently, but just the touch of his soft denim clothing against her skin was like fire.

'Damned little fool,' he muttered in her ear. 'Lie still or you'll make it worse than it is already.' And she did lie still as he shouldered his way into the house, moving straight to the bathroom.

'Right, in you go,' he growled. And in she went, the pain now so intense that even his voice hurt, although not so much as the first blast of water when he turned on the cold tap.

The water was cold only in comparison to the reddened flush of her skin; she already knew there was no such thing as truly cold tap water in Port Hedland during summer. But her sunburn was nothing when compared to the blistering heat of Wade's tongue as he proceeded to abuse her for being so damned stupid.

'I should have known you'd pull something like this,' he charged. 'Where the hell were you when they were handing out the brains, hiding behind the door?'

Futile to argue, even if she'd had the strength. And she didn't. If it hadn't been for him holding her, she was quite certain she'd have crumpled into a heap on the floor of the shower stall.

Wade seemed oblivious to the soaking of his own clothes as he stood in the shower with her, turning her this way and that, directing the stream of lukewarm water across every portion of her sunburned body.

Holly was like a shop-window mannequin, silently allowing her body to be manoeuvred as he wished.

Her mind was numb, unable to find the words for any sort of argument, uncaring as he kept up a running commentary, most of it uncomplimentary to say the least. Odd words crept into her consciousness, words like *idiot*, *bloody Pom*, *no brains*, and yet other words, too, like *lovely* and *exquisite*. None could maintain a place in her aching, confused mind.

Wade worked with consummate gentleness, holding her steady with one hand as he soothingly applied soft, liquid soap, then rinsed it carefully away again, his fingers like moth wings on her sun-sensitised skin.

'Right, that'll have to do,' he said finally, and lifted her out on to the cool, tiled floor. 'Reckon you can stand?'

Holly nodded a yes, or at least he thought she did, because he let her go and began drying her off. And still with that incredible gentleness, the towel dabbing, patting, soaking up the water without abrading her sunburn.

Finished, finally, he stood off and surveyed her, his eyes taking in every detail. And Holly knew, somehow, that he was seeing not only the sun's ravages, but all the softness, each curve and hollow of her figure.

And for one, single instant, so fleeting that she thought she'd imagined it, there was something in his eyes that was as gentle as his touch, a look that was a total caress, filled not with lust or wanting or needing, but simply of love. But it was too quick to be caught, too elusive to be sure of.

Then his eyes were their normal icy green, not really angry, perhaps even slightly compassionate, but certainly not loving.

'Now comes the fun part,' he muttered in what was almost a growl. 'Good thing you're not ridiculously modest.'

And before Holly could catch his meaning, the top of the bikini was unfastened, whipped away from her to reveal two tiny patches of white at the end of her breasts and the thin white lines where the ties had been.

'Don't fuss,' he snapped as she cringed away from him. 'I just had to be sure you weren't wearing one of those damned tan-thru things; and just as well you weren't, or you'd be in real trouble; sunburned nipples are no joke.'

'You ... you might have asked,' Holly stammered, attempting to cover herself with her hands, yet realising it was a silly, useless gesture. He'd already seen her, indeed had seen her breasts before, had kissed them, touched them intimately. There was nothing intimate in his attitude now, however.

He shook his head, not sadly, but in the manner of a scolding parent. 'You'd better hope my sunburn remedy works, young lady, or you'll be spending the next three days on your feet. Now stand still; I'm not going to hurt you.'

Holly did as she was told, but she closed her eyes as he prowled round her in a circle, alternately shaking the huge aerosol can of sunburn spray and directing it on to her body in sweeping bursts of cool agony.

His fingers were undeniably gentle as he rubbed it in, slowly but without a hint of sensuality, although she could somehow tell also that his touch wasn't totally impersonal. Then he sprayed on another layer.

'Right. I'm afraid you're going to have to stay sitting up for a bit, long enough for that to really soak in,' he said. 'How do you feel now, sick? Headache? Tell me the truth, too, and don't underplay it because it's important.'

'A ... a bit of a headache, but I'm not going to be sick or anything, I don't think,' she replied shakily. 'I just feel really weak and ... and a bit dizzy.'

'Hummmmph,' he muttered. 'Well, we'll take your temperature just to be sure, and if that's okay then some salt tablets are probably in order. I think you've just got a bit too much sun, although not enough for sunstroke or anything really serious. With skin as fair as yours, I'm surpised it isn't worse.'

He slipped the top of her bikini into place with unexpected expertise, then commanded her to open her mouth and receive the thermometer beneath her tongue. She endured his ministrations without complaint, even gagging down the bitter salt tablets he prescribed.

She let him lead her to the lounge, already feeling much recovered but certainly not enough to argue. Only when he directed her to sit down in a cloth-covered armchair did she demur, only to be told, 'Don't be stupid; it'll wash.'

'That's hardly the point,' she replied. 'Surely it would be just as easy to cover it first with a towel or something.'

'You are the most argumentative, stubborn female I've ever met,' he replied. 'Even worse then Jessica, and I'd never have thought that possible.'

But he did get her the towel, and even spread it over the chair before helping Holly position herself as comfortably as she could, under the circumstances.

The anaesthetic properties of the spray were taking effect, and apart from the remains of her headache, she felt almost normal. But the redness of her skin assured her it would be days, perhaps, before she finished paying for her folly.

'I'm really sorry,' she said, certain that her apology wouldn't be accepted, yet equally certain it was required. 'I honestly did take care. I wasn't out for long, and I stayed in the shade almost all the time. Honestly.'

And was astonished when he replied. 'I'm sure you

did, but the shade is deceptive. You can be burned just from reflected light up here in the north—even in the shade.'

Her eyes must have shown her disbelief, because he met her gaze and laughed. 'True! You probably got the worst of your burn *after* you lay down in the hammock, when you thought you were safe. I've done it myself.'

That, Holly decided, was probably a lie. She couldn't imagine Wade Bannister ever doing anything so stupid as getting an unexpected sunburn. Certainly not in recent years, at any rate. His skin had that rich, lustrous bronze tone that bespoke long exposure to the sun.

'Well I still feel rather foolish,' she replied. 'Typical tourist, although I realise that's no excuse.'

'With your complexion, I'd have thought you'd have learned about sunburn years ago, even in England,' he said. 'You've got the most beautiful skin I've ever seen; makes me think of strawberries and cream.'

Holly giggled, confused slightly by the unexpected compliment. 'The expression is supposed to be peaches and cream, although right now I suppose you're closer with strawberries. Thank you.'

His reply seemed gruff by comparison. 'Well just see that you take more care after this. I'll pick up some sunscreen this afternoon, and I want your promise that you'll use it. Religiously! Skin cancer is no joke, and Australia's got the worst record in the world, especially in the tropics.'

'I promise,' she said. And meant it. Then she shivered, for the first time aware of the coolness created by the air-conditioning.

'Stomach playing up, or is it just the chills?' he asked, eyes narrowing in concern. Was he truly concerned, Holly wondered, or just returning to being his usual officious self?

'It's nothing, I'm sure,' she replied, but when she

stood up she was strangely light-headed, the room seemed to shimmer like heat waves around her. She swayed, would have fallen, but his hands closed round her waist, pulling her close as he swept her into his arms with the descent of oblivion.

And he was still there when she returned to consciousness, her eyes slowly opening to settle first on the lean, tall figure sprawled comfortably in the arm chair near the foot of her bed, a book open in his lap.

'Feeling better?' he asked, a grin playing about his wide, mobile mouth. 'The first thing you'll want is a drink, I bet. Don't get up ... I'll bring it.'

He was gone before Holly could say a word, returning a moment later with a tall, frosted glass of lemonade which he handed down to her with a flourish.

Holly sat up; the action was necessary if she was to drink from the glass, and she was pleased to find her dizziness gone. She could still feel the tingling of her skin, but her head was now clear and she felt almost normal.

Wade raised one eyebrow. 'It'll be a light supper for you tonight, I reckon,' he said. 'Scrambled eggs? Omelette?'

'Oh, look ... I'll fix something,' she protested, but she might just as well have saved her breath.

'Best I do it. The way you're going today, you'd only end up burning the house down,' he replied, but had the grace, at least, to blunt the barb of the remark with a smile. 'I've got a few things to do right now, but you stay and rest if you'd like. Come on out whenever you're ready.'

And he was gone with a nod that might have been brusque had he not been smiling. It was, she noted, the kind of indulgent smile reserved for wayward children, or was that her conscience judging?

Holly finished the drink and leaned back against her

pillow, unable not to wonder if Wade Bannister's attitude mightn't be mellowing slightly. Or was it just because she was at a strong disadvantage? Somehow she knew he wasn't the type to knowingly take unfair advantage, at least not according to his own rules.

The trouble was, she didn't know his rules. Even thinking the worst of her, he'd made a very close attempt at seduction, which somehow didn't fit in with what she'd imagined his thinking to be. How could he possibly desire a woman he detested?

But then, how could he be so considerate to a silly, sunburned, stupid tourist? And he had been—was being—very considerate. She couldn't deny that. Or, she mused, was he setting her up for something? That, too, was vaguely possible and not totally out of character. Wade Bannister could be a very devious person, when he chose.

He wasn't in evidence when Holly finally emerged, a light silken wrap gathered closely about her body in a shroud that seemed only to contain the sunburn heat she was producing. And five minutes later she was convinced he'd left the house entirely, though she'd no idea where.

She was equally convinced she could no longer bear the touch of the silk against her flushed skin, so she returned to her room to change to a pair of shorts and a light halter top. When she emerged a second time, he was standing beside the lounge bar, a tall glass in his hand.

'I'd suggest something soft for you,' he said, 'at least until tomorrow, when we can judge how serious an injury you've really done yourself.'

Holly paused uncertainly, on the verge of telling him she rarely drank anything stronger than beer or wine anyway. But he probably wouldn't believe her, and now that he'd had his say, she perversely wanted something else, even though she could at least recognise her own contrariness.

'I don't suppose I could have a beer?' she asked, keeping the question non-committal, non-aggressive. And watched as one dark eyebrow raised in a silent query of her minor defiance.

'We'll compromise. You can have a shandy,' he finally said, and immediately began pouring beer into a half-glass of lemonade, foaming up the brew into a frothy head.

Holly dismissed her natural inclination to argue; surely she'd done enough of that already today, without deliberately going out of her way to be difficult. Instead, she sipped gratefully at the foaming drink, then smiled her acceptance.

'What are *you* drinking?' she asked after a moment, not really caring, but finding the silence seemed to hum round in her head, creating a noise of its own. Silence made her too aware of the tall man who leaned casually against the bar, made it too possible for him to be aware of her skimpy costume as he eyed the marks of the sun on her legs and midriff.

Wade glanced down at his glass, almost as if he had to think about a reply. 'Soda water,' he finally said. 'I'm probably the only person in the entire Northwest who can't stop a thirst with beer. I like it, no mistake, but not when I'm really thirsty.'

And the silence swarmed back around them, so loud it made Holly want to put down her glass and flee to the sanctuary of her room. How could she stand to stay here with him if he wouldn't even talk to her?

'What are you thinking about that makes you frown so much?'

The question was totally unexpected, especially as she hadn't thought he was in the mood for conversation.

Neither did she realise she'd been frowning, and Holly quickly re-arranged her face.

'I was just wondering about Jessica,' she replied, lying and sure he knew it. 'I don't think she told me the truth about these tests she's having; I think it's much more serious than she's letting on.'

'It is, although it could be a lot worse,' Wade admitted. And then, after a moment, 'And I suppose you're not overjoyed at being stuck here with me, either?'

Now what did that mean? Holly tried to keep her voice absolutely calm. 'I . . . would prefer Jessica, but so long as you . . .'

'Keep my hands to myself?' And his grin was unfathomable. 'Let's just say, dear Holly, that you're as safe with me as you want to be.'

Which meant she wasn't safe at all, but Holly knew he must never know that. 'Then I'm totally safe,' she said with a brightness she didn't feel.

Wade stared deliberately at her sunburn, his expression making it quite clear what he was looking at. 'For a few days you are; that's for sure,' he said with a sudden grin. 'You would be safe from anybody until that sunburn wears off.'

'How serious is Jessica's condition, really?' Holly replied in a deliberate change of subject. Discussing her safety or lack of it with the only man who could threaten it wasn't her idea of a reasonable discussion. Besides, she knew that Jessica hadn't been totally successful in fooling Wade about her situation. Obviously he cared a great deal for her aunt, and wasn't likely to be fobbed off by false assertions.

'She could very easily require heart surgery. And there's a chance she could as easily die, with or without it,' he replied soberly, his face showing that he got no pleasure from the bluntness, yet saw no sense in hiding the truth.

'Oh my G ... I wish you'd told me earlier. I should be with her!' Holly cried, and her voice raised in anger at the bland, negative shake of his head.

'No. She's too damned proud and independent for that,' he said, and Holly recognised that as the truth. 'She got you here knowing the situation herself, but there is no way on earth she wants either of *us* to know it, so I think we must respect that, at least for the moment,' he said.

'And these tests?' Holly didn't, couldn't argue with his logic.

'They could be the prelude to open-heart surgery, but not yet, I think. At any rate, she's in the best hands possible and she'll have the best of care. We'll just have to see.'

'You've made sure of that, haven't you?' she asked, not expecting an answer because she already knew. Wade was one step ahead of Jessica all the way. He was the type who always would be.

Whatever his reply might have been, it was forestalled by the ringing of the telephone, an insistent jangling in the relative quiet of the house. The one-sided conversation that followed meant less than nothing to Holly. It was a jumble of technical shorthand and jargon she couldn't begin to understand.

'Well, that solves part of your problem, anyway,' he said immediately after ringing off. 'I'll be leaving in the morning for a few days, maybe longer. Do you think you can manage to hang on here by yourself?'

'Until Jessica comes back? Certainly,' she replied. 'Unless of course there's a cyclone. I'd like you to brief me on that eventuality before you go. Jessica did, of course, but I'd like to be more sure.' She felt a great surge of relief in knowing she wouldn't have to continue walking on egg-shells indefinitely. Knowing the instinctive attraction she seemed to have for Wade, she could only imagine difficulties if they were too long together alone. And yet, well, she'd have to ignore that. Her feelings for him were too new, too startling.

'There isn't much to know except pure common sense,' he was saying. 'The house is pretty well okay, just make sure there's nothing lying around loose outside and make sure *you* stay inside, where it's relatively safe. But really, I wouldn't worry a whole lot about it. The long-range forecast doesn't show anything to cause much of a problem.'

They were having dinner, a light, gentle dinner of poached eggs on toast—Wade's suggestion and Wade's cooking—when the telephone interrupted a second time. And this time it was only too easy for Holly to follow the conversation; he made sure of that!

'Of course everything's all right here, Jess,' he said almost immediately. 'Holly? Well I'll let you speak to her in a minute and you can judge for yourself.'

But he didn't turn the telephone over to Holly immediately. Not even soon. Instead, he talked on and on to Jessica, while Holly fumed with indignation at being able to hear only half the conversation. It was pleasing that Wade was obviously wording his own comments to give her as much information as possible, but it wasn't enough; she wanted to talk to Jessica herself.

'You'll be back tomorrow?' she cried once he'd finally passed the phone on with a grin. 'Will you really? Does that mean everything's all right?'

'Not that simple, I'm afraid,' was the disturbing reply. 'I'll have to come back in a week or so, and take things very easy in the interim, but then I hope, things will be just fine.'

'But . . . it hardly seems worth flying all the way back for such a short time,' Holly said, shooting Wade a furious glance as she spoke. 'Couldn't you just, well, stay there? I'm really worried about you flying.'

Wade shrugged his shoulders, clearly indicating the uselessness, in his view, of argument with her aunt. 'No, that wouldn't be suitable at all,' Jessica was saying. 'I'll be far more comfortable at home, and really, what's the sense of you coming all the way from England if we can't spend as much time as possible together? No, I'll be back on the first flight tomorrow.'

Wade hardly kept still until Holly had finished her talk and hung up the telephone. 'Damn that woman!' he growled. 'She's lying about something; I know it. What is it with the women in your family, anyway? They couldn't lie straight in bed.'

Holly's involuntary gasp of protest was snowed under by his voice, harsh now with emotion and his obvious, genuine love and concern for Jessica.

'When she gets over this, she's going to hear from me,' he growled. 'I'm getting sick and tired of you women thinking I'm so stupid I'll believe the flimsiest of lies. If she wasn't so sick, I'd wait until she got home tomorrow and take her over my knee, that's what!'

'Well you don't have to scream at me about it. It isn't my fault,' Holly replied.

'Nobody's screaming at you. I'm just giving you fair warning, so if you see me going after Jess one day with a great stick you'll know why.'

'I'll do better than that; I'll probably help you catch her,' Holly replied with a grin. Now that she knew he wasn't serious, but was only blowing off steam, she suddenly felt much more relaxed. She rather liked *this* Wade Bannister; the outburst made him almost human, less remote.

'Just so long as we get the chance, that's all I ask,' he replied with a grin of his own, then reached up to thrust back a lock of brown hair that had fallen across his forehead. 'Anyway, young Holly, I suggest you trot off to bed now. I've got a few calls to make—I'd like to rearrange things so I can also be there when Jess arrives, just to see how she looks—and then I think I'll nod off too. It's been a long day for both of us.'

'All right. I'll just tidy up here first,' Holly said, and began to gather up the dinner dishes. And somehow she wasn't surprised when Wade stepped in to help her, so that the dishes were cleaned up and put away in only a few minutes.

'Right. Now off to bed with you,' he said, bending to place a light, almost brotherly kiss on her forehead.

The memory of that kiss, strangely, remained until after Holly had wakened next morning to find her sunburn much improved and her mind clear and alert.

Wade, also, seemed to have rested well. He was sitting at the kitchen table when she entered the room, a cup of coffee in front of him and the makings of a gargantuan breakfast spread out on the kitchen counter.

'If you're as hungry as I am, it still may not be enough,' he grinned. 'But pour yourself some coffee first; I'll start cooking in a minute.'

Each of them, Holly thought, ate enough breakfast to keep two full-grown men working for a day, but it was a strangely silent if totally convivial meal. And as on the evening before, Wade helped her to tidy up, then disappeared into his own quarters to shower and change for his working day.

He was waiting when she had finished getting ready for the trip to the airport, dressed casually but tidily in khaki and wearing strongly made work boots with thick soles.

'I won't be coming back here with you,' he said, 'so we'll have to take both vehicles to the airport and then you can drive Jess back. I should be back myself, oh, within a couple of days, anyway.'

Both vehicles. That explained how he'd arrived the

day before without her knowing he'd even come to Port Hedland. And sure enough, when they walked through to the garage, an elderly, somewhat battered Land Rover squatted beside the sleek station sedan.

Festooned with equipment, it looked like something out of a desert war movie, but no worse than many of the vehicles Holly had seen during her tour of the town. Rugged, go-anywhere machines obviously must have a place in this climate and terrain, she realised. And rugged, go-anywhere men, as well.

Holly found herself idly wondering, as she followed the big truck on the long drive to the airport, what it would be like to travel into the vastness of the wilderness which seemed to surround Port Hedland. Rough, certainly, and yet surely there must be compensations apart from the obvious mineral wealth.

It was such an old land, and yet the touch of man's hand upon it was—certainly by European standards— so very new. She had noticed in the tourist literature she'd collected that Dutch sea captain Dirk Hartog was thought to be the first European to land in Australia, in Shark Bay, about halfway down the coast towards Perth. That was 1616, modern times by the terms of her own country's development.

And yet, much of what he had seen must have been virtually identical to the landscape over which she'd flown only days before. A vast, seemingly empty wilderness with hardly a sign that the twentieth century had arrived.

And what did Wade Bannister see, whenever he 'went bush'? Did he see only the modern, the development potential, or was there an adventurer's soul that also saw the past, the vastness? She thought that one day, perhaps, she might ask him.

Jessica, when she stepped down from the aircraft and scuttled for the shade of the airport, looked better than when she'd left, Holly thought. Her colour, certainly, was much improved, and she walked just a bit straighter, smiled just a bit wider.

'You're an old fraud,' Wade grinned as he stepped forward to greet her. 'You didn't go south for any tests; you were just wallowing in the fleshpots.'

'How I wish it were true,' Jessica replied. 'And from the colour of Holly's face I should have taken her with me. What have you two been up to?'

Holly waited until she'd clasped her aunt in a gentle hug before attempting a reply, but Wade beat her to it. 'Holly just found out that being a sun goddess isn't all it's cracked up to be,' he chuckled, then laughed outright as Holly actually managed a blush that outshone her sunburn.

'Anyway, I can't stay and chat. I'm supposed to be at Marble Bar, working, not entertaining ladies, no matter how eminently entertainable.'

'Well before you go, I'd certainly like two minutes of your precious time,' Jessica replied, obviously not at all intimidated by his show of authority. 'What about this party on Friday night? Do you have anything special in mind, or can Holly and I just plan it as we please?'

Wade frowned, the move thrusting deep creases down his tanned face. 'I thought under the circumstances we'd forget about it,' he began. 'After all, you're supposed to be taking it easy.'

'And I shall, although not if I have to spend the next two days retracting all the invitations,' Jessica replied pertly.

'Now hang on. There are forty or fifty people involved. You oughtn't to be mucking about catering to a crowd like that.'

'I don't intend to. Or at least not totally. Holly will help, of course, and . . .'

'And without taking anything away from Holly,

you'll still end up overworking yourself, because that's your way,' he interrupted. 'I'm not sure even the two of us could manage to keep you under control, and as it is, I mightn't get back with time to do more than shower, change and start playing gracious host. I tell you, Jess, I don't think much of the idea.'

'And that's just because you're a typical chauvinist,' was the unexpected reply. 'You just can't understand how easy it is to cater for forty or fifty people, especially if we just do a monster barbecue. There's the big barbecue spit, and I've time to arrange for a pig if I get on to the butcher straight away. The rest is only a few potatoes and a few salads; no work in that.'

Wade wasn't happy, but he could see, Holly thought, that this was one argument he must lose. 'Oh, all right,' he finally muttered. 'But I want it clearly understood— you use disposable everything, knives, forks, plates, glasses, the lot. And Holly, if she doesn't damned well take things easy enough to suit you, then shut the whole effort down. I don't care whose feelings get hurt. And don't overwork yourself, either; is that clear?'

'Abundantly,' she replied, meeting his gaze with her own eyes shining with thanks. She knew how difficult it must be for him, yet both of them realised arguing with Jessica wasn't the way to keep her relaxed and calm. Better if Holly at least tried to take charge, and with Wade's support do her best to ensure that Jessica was forced to take things easy.

Her aunt, however, seemed quite prepared to accept the new arrangements. 'I do hereby promise not to overwork,' she solemnly declared, 'especially after seeing what happened to Alan Mason. You'll remember the attack he suffered during the party you attended?' she said to a shocked and suddenly wary Holly, 'well he apparently had another one the very next day! True,' she continued, apparently thinking Holly's astonished look was understandable, 'he was in hospital the same time I was, with a broken nose, a black eye and several broken ribs. He apparently blacked out and fell down some stairs.'

CHAPTER FIVE

HOLLY had to take a deep breath before she even dared look up at Wade, wondering as she did so if he could even bring himself to meet her eyes.

Another attack the very next day! Astonishing, especially considering the nature of Alan Mason's first *attack*. Even more astonishing, considering that only she and Wade knew the exact nature of that first *attack*.

But whatever she expected to see in Wade's eyes, it wasn't the calm, bland expression of total innocence that met her own fiery gaze. He looked straight into her eyes, his own like ocean-deep pools of still, fathomless green ice.

'I think the grog must be getting to Alan,' he said in a voice notable only for what it didn't reveal.

'Well, that wouldn't surprise me,' Jessica piped up, seeming oblivious to the aura of awareness that hung between Wade and Holly like some tangible, almost visible cloud. 'Alan Mason never could hold his liquor, and he's got worse over the past few years.'

Holly nearly gasped. Her immediate question, one that she could, of course, never ask, was whether Ramona Mason's father might have at some time made a pass at Jessica, too.

It wasn't beyond the bounds of reason. Her aunt was still, even taking into account her illness, an exceptionally striking woman, and if Mason had been a business associate of Wade's, they must surely have crossed paths on various occasions.

But there was another question that seemed far more important, especially since it seemed clear Wade wasn't going to give her any answers, and Holly found herself unable to keep from considering it after Wade's departure and their own dispersal for the long drive home.

What had *really* happened to Alan Mason? Only Wade, Holly, and the man himself knew the true nature of his first attack, so what of the second one, occurring so very, very coincidentally the very next day? He could, indeed, have really blacked out and fallen down some stairs, but the reported injuries sounded suspiciously specific and not truly in line with logic. Wasn't there a saying that drunks couldn't hurt themselves falling?

Holly would have bet money that Wade Bannister had something to do with Alan Mason's attack, but if he had, he obviously wasn't going to say so, and certainly she didn't dare ask. Not in front of Aunt Jessica, at any rate. It would mean too many explanations of a type she didn't care to become involved in.

And her sunburn was creating quite enough explanations, Holly found as her aunt questioned her about that on the trip home. She managed, she thought, to pass off the incident as being totally trivial, but Jessica was shrewd, far too shrewd, for Holly's taste.

Just as well that Wade was going off 'bush' for several days. With all three of them in the same house, it would take very little time indeed for her aunt to deduce Holly's growing feelings for the man, and since they were feelings that must be quite unrequited, they must be kept at a level that didn't make Jessica either suspicious or overly optimistic about the future success of her matchmaking.

'I'm certainly pleased that you didn't suffer too severe a burn, Holly,' her aunt said. 'I feel quite badly about it, because it's something I certainly should have warned you about.'

'It's something I shouldn't have *had* to be warned about,' Holly replied. 'But, as you say, I was lucky to get off so lightly. I'll know better next time.'

'Of course you will, dear. It's like so many other aspects of living up here; it's mostly common sense and I know you've plenty of that.'

'Even if Wade ... Mr Bannister isn't so sure,' Holly replied. 'Not that I blame him, actually. It must have given him quite a shock to return home to find a lobster in his hammock.'

'Not if his memories are still good,' Jessica replied with a chuckle. 'I seem to remember doing almost exactly the same thing during the first week I was here, and *I* certainly should have known better, having spent several years in Darwin before I came to work for Wade.'

'*You* did something as silly as that? Oh, I can't believe that,' Holly laughed. 'And certainly Mr Bannister couldn't have remembered or he'd have said something, I'm sure. He, well, he certainly went out of his way to put me at ease about the whole thing, I must say.'

'Oh, he would. Wade is one of the gentlest men I've ever encountered,' Jessica said. To which Holly almost laughed aloud, thinking of Alan Mason's second incident and her own interpretation of what must really have happened. Or was she reading too much circumstantial evidence into it? The Wade Bannister she knew would, without question, have physically chastised Alan Mason—but only if he were totally certain it was deserved. Which, as she remembered, he hadn't been at all.

'I'm certainly glad to see that you two seem to be getting along better than you originally expected,' Jessica said, interrupting Holly's thoughts. 'I ... I really must admit, Holly, that I had hoped you would. I know your feelings about matchmaking, and yet ... well ...'

'Well—nothing! Somebody your age, if you don't mind me throwing that into it, should know very well you can't mix apples and oranges,' Holly replied gravely. 'I am not Wade Bannister's type and he certainly isn't mine, thank you very much, but we shall get along comfortably enough while I'm here. Anything beyond that is purely in your imagination and I wish you'd accept that.'

'Oh, I do,' Jessica replied, and promptly lapsed into a silence that lasted the duration of their journey home.

Once home, thankfully, she immediately pleaded tiredness from her journey and retired for a rest, giving Holly a reprieve from the inquisition she knew must eventually come.

Did Holly like Wade Bannister? I love him. Did Holly not think he was handsome? I think he's breathtaking. Did Holly not think they were compatible? Definitely not!

And that evening, Holly began to wish that Jessica *had* got stuck into such an inquisition—which she didn't—instead of throwing herself headlong into the preparations for Friday's party.

They spent the evening organising the requirements of the guest list, accommodation for those from outside Port Hedland, transportation for those who might require it, a general plan of attack for the party as a whole. It was Tuesday night, which didn't really leave them a lot of time, but surely it was enough, Holly thought, that Jessica needn't get quite so involved.

'I am not overdoing anything,' her aunt insisted. 'The secret of good entertaining is good planning; planning may be time consuming, but it isn't and shouldn't be stressful.'

'But you should be back in bed,' Holly finally said. 'It's ten o'clock and I, for one, am very tired indeed. So please can we leave it until morning?'

'Only if you accept that no matter what Wade says, I will not accept being molly-coddled,' Jessica replied sternly. 'I am not an invalid and I am not a child.'

'No, you're just a stubborn old woman who's far too used to having her own way,' Holly replied just as peevishly. 'And I am here to tell you, dear Aunt Jessica, that it won't work with me. You're supposed to be taking things easy and I intend to make very, very certain that you do. Now will you please—*please*—stop arguing and pack it in for tonight?'

Jessica grudgingly relented, and after she'd gone off to bed Holly sat down over a cup of hot chocolate, her head in her hands as she wondered if either of them could survive the next few days. Already, she could fully sympathise with Wade's anger towards her aunt and the woman's refusal to slow down, to accept that her refusal to admit to being ill might even be dangerous.

And if anything happened to Jessica now, while—at least in Wade's opinion—she was under Holly's care . . . 'He'd never forgive me, not that I'd be able to forgive myself,' she muttered aloud.

When she, herself, finally went to bed, Holly slept poorly. She kept having visions of the next three days being one long, continuous confrontation with Jessica's stubbornness, and seemed to lie awake most of the night dreaming up ways to combat it without forcing a hurtful confrontation.

But in the morning, she found a changed Jessica, a reasonable woman miraculously resigned to her situation and no longer so ready to ignore her fragile health.

'I'm sorry about last night,' she said almost immediately upon entering the kitchen where Holly was sipping at her coffee. 'You're right; I am a stubborn old woman, and you were even more right to put me in my place.'

'You're an old fraud is what you are,' Holly laughed. 'You know very well that your Mr Bannister will quite likely phone today, and you just want me able to say that you've behaved.'

'He's an extremely busy man; it wouldn't do to have him worrying about nothing,' Jessica replied. 'Of course, he'll worry anyway because he's that type, but I wouldn't want him to think, well . . .'

'Well then you won't mind promising to behave? Not just today, but right through until this party is over and done with, in fact, until you're through the next batch of tests, so we know for sure just how serious your condition is?' Holly kept her voice calm, but the determination wasn't hidden. She would get control of this situation now, she vowed.

'Oh, all right. I will promise,' Jessica agreed. 'But just remember that I won't put up with being excluded completely, either. This is to be *our* party, and I do want it to go off well.'

'Nobody wants to exclude you; what I want is to be sure you're in fit shape to attend the party,' Holly retorted. 'Which means that you do the planning and I do the work. And, you get plenty of rest.'

Her severity seemed to work, too. Jessica was remarkably subdued during the rest of the day. Holly organised the whole pig for the spit roast, whipped into town to purchase the vast quantities of disposable plates, glasses and cutlery they'd need, along with a variety of decorations, arranged for the hire of several trestle tables and folding chairs, bought enough potatoes, she thought, to feed a regiment, and returned home to find her aunt resting, which rather surprised her.

The biggest surprise, however, was contained in Wade's telephone call that evening from Marble Bar.

'How is the old dragon? Giving you any trouble?'

Those were his first two questions, and the grunted acceptance of Holly's replies—'Okay' and 'Not really'—didn't give her a lot of satisfaction. It didn't sound as if he believed her, just for starters.

She was more voluble in describing how well the party plans were going, but from his replies she got the feeling he was preoccupied, a feeling that was later confirmed when he asked to speak to Jessica. The aunt's replies left little unsaid.

'A house-guest and helper? Well, I suppose it wouldn't hurt, although certainly we have everything almost under control now anyway. Of course we have room; that's not an issue at all. Well, it certainly isn't necessary, but if you insist.'

The strained expression on her aunt's face both shocked and surprised Holly, but the greatest shock came when Jessica put down the telephone and said, 'Ramona Mason will be arriving tomorrow morning to give us a hand.'

As it turned out, that was the understatement of the year. When Ramona alighted from a taxi late next morning, equipped with enough luggage for a six-month stay, it was immediately clear that she had no intention of giving anyone a hand—she intended to take over entirely.

'Of course, what you've done so far is, well, all right. As far as it goes,' she said after being installed in a bedroom conveniently just across the hall from Wade's. 'But really, this business of paper plates and *plastic* glasses. Well it just won't do. There are important people coming to this party, people who simply shouldn't be expected to drink champagne from *plastic* glasses.

Jessica took the easy course. She pleaded her ill-health and stayed out of it as much as possible. Holly had no such excuse.

The issue of the glasses turned out to be one of the less important, and by that evening Holly would have sold her soul for any excuse to avoid Ramona's involvement in what had been planned as a relatively simple party.

There was nothing Ramona could do to change the spit-roasted pig concept, but that was about the only aspect of the party which remained inviolate. The blonde found fault with every bit of Holly and Jessica's planning, generally on the excuse that the visitors to the party were 'important' and therefore deserved only the best.

Wade's concept of beer, white wine and/or orange juice was among the first to go. There would be beer, of course, but only for what Ramona termed 'those few with common tastes'. Using Wade's credit facilities as if they were her own—and giving everyone the impression that if they were not, they soon would be—she ordered champagne by the magnum, spirits by the case, and hired a complete range of plates, glasses, cutlery and trimmings to match.

The trestle tables must be covered in fine table-clothes—'You'll see to that, of course, Miss Grange'— and of course there must be sufficient shade. And certainly there would have to be a wide, complete range of canapés and hors d'oeuvres.

She took great delight, although never—Holly noticed—in Jessica's hearing, in muttering about the folly of entrusting party planning to one's housekeeping staff, and alienated everyone at the town's best hotel by re-arranging accommodation arrangements for those people arriving from elsewhere.

Holly found her own role shrinking to that of unpaid, unwanted housemaid, and spent most of the last two days washing, ironing, dusting and cleaning, while Ramona swanned about like some exotic southern belle in a poor American movie.

'I may kill her,' she confided to Jessica when she paused for a breather and a brief visit. 'Slowly ... painfully.'

'Not worth the trouble,' was the surprisingly bright reply. 'I'd just give her enough rope and let her do it herself. She's bound to, sooner or later.'

'Not soon enough. Last week wouldn't be soon enough,' Holly replied with a great gnashing of her perfect teeth. 'I have just never *seen* such unmitigated gall, never in all my life. That woman is ... well, she's just unbelievable.'

Holly had just spent two hours rearranging various potted plants in the garden area—potted plants hired by Ramona and arranged, re-arranged and further re-arranged by Holly at Ramona's instructions.

It had been difficult to hold her temper, especially when Ramona took every opportunity to criticise, but Holly fought and managed—just barely—to keep from blowing up.

The only saving grace of the entire situation was the pig and the myriad preparations that were needed if it was to become the centrepiece for the party. Pigs, for whatever reason, did not come under Ramona's inflated sense of responsibility.

She took one look at the carcass, which arrived first thing on the Friday morning complete with head, tail and trotters, and shudderingly left the kitchen to Holly and Jessica.

'I'm sure you can manage,' was Ramona's departing comment as she cast a hateful glance over one chic shoulder before going out to finish her flower arrangements.

'I know we could manage—especially if it was her on the spit instead of this splendid fellow,' Jessica muttered. 'Couldn't you just see her with an apple in her mouth, turning gently over the flames?'

Holly had to laugh, although her feelings were quite in harmony with Jessica's.

'It's tempting, but Wade would never forgive us for maybe poisoning his guests,' she muttered as they struggled to fit the clamps that would hold the four-foot-long beast to the spit. The fire in Wade's huge spit-roast had been going for several hours, so as to provide a deep bed of coals for the roasting of the pig, but keeping the fire going was the least of the work.

They first washed the pig, then spent a long time slicing intricate designs through the skin to provide the crisp but juicy crackling that would surround the tender meat. After the apple-and-raisin stuffing was correctly positioned, the pig was wrapped in a layer of chicken wire, then several layers of foil, and a final wrapping of wire to keep the foil in place.

Only then could it be placed over the fire and the electric spit turned on to begin its six-hour rotating journey, timed to finish at approximately seven o'clock that evening.

'It could be an hour either way, or worse,' Jessica muttered. 'I'm positive that beast was bigger than the last one we did, but that was nearly a year ago, so I can't be sure. If there was only Wade to please, it probably wouldn't matter, but I expect dear Miss Mason will go all strange and excitable if dinner isn't ready precisely on time.'

The heat of the day, combined with the heat created by the enormous roasting apparatus, made it impossible for Jessica to supervise the spit-roast except by coming out occasionally for a check on the fire. It was left to Holly to keep the flames at just the right height to make sure the pig was cooking at the proper speed. Ramona managed to stay as far away from the fire as possible, although she managed one or two caustic comments about the operation from a careful distance.

As the afternoon wore on, the temperature rising into the high thirties, Holly wished desperately that she could retreat to the coolness of the air-conditioning, or at the very least take time out for a shower. She was wearing only a light cotton blouse, now so damp with perspiration it might as well have been worn in the shower, and a pair of old shorts that looked little better.

Through the glass patio doors, she could see Ramona, looking as cool as Holly was hot, swanning about in a light, swirling gown with a tall, cool drink in one hand and a cigarette in the other. Jessica, at least, was able to retreat to the sanctuary of the granny flat, and Holly was tempted once or twice to just walk away from the rotating spit and join her.

Whenever Ramona chanced to glance outside, her very expression made it clear what she thought of Holly's outfit. And, indeed, of my presence here in the first place, Holly thought, barely resisting at one point the urge to stick out her tongue at the chilly blonde.

She had thought that during the final hour of cooking she might be able to slip in, have a shower, and change into something more appropriate for the party, but it was not to be. That last cooking period turned out to be the one in which the pig began to drip small quantities of fat, fat which would immediately flare up into tiny volcanoes of sizzling heat from the lava-like bed of coals.

Instead of going to change, Holly found herself constantly busy with the garden sprayer, using it like a water pistol to control the flare-ups, to keep the flames from scorching the slowly rotating animal.

To make matters worse, the aroma of the roasting pork was increasing, clawing forth groans of agony from her own empty stomach.

'We'll have to have that foil off, I reckon,' Jessica said during a brief visit. 'Usually, that's Wade's job, but as he isn't here. I guess we'll just have to manage it by ourselves.'

By the time that was accomplished, Holly was just as glad she hadn't taken time to shower and change. She was pork fat from finger-tip to elbows, and had it splattered liberally along her thighs and across her blouse and shorts.

It took all of both their strengths to lift the spit and its burden away from the fire, cut away the wire and foil, and then replace the pig once again over the fire.

'I think I'll have to clean up my act,' Holly remarked at that point. 'If hell's anything like this, I doubt I could stand it.'

The answer came not from Jessica, who stood silent from the strain of lifting, but from the strident voice of Ramona Mason, who had chosen that particular moment to emerge on one of her periodic tours of inspection.

'My goodness,' she remarked caustically. 'Whatever are you planning to do with all this wire and tinfoil? It'll have to be disposed of, you realise, and quickly! The first guests are due any minute.'

Holly refrained from telling the blonde what she might do with the rubbish, and instead lifted it herself, carrying the mess around to where she could deposit it in rubbish bins out of sight of the party.

Only to find herself dashing back to man the sprayer as hot pork drippings flared up into a minor bonfire beneath the succulently browning pig.

Moments later, the chiming of the door bell announced the first of their visitors, but Holly, by this time, was past caring. 'I'd feel like Cinderella, if I had the time,' she muttered, jetting another shot of water to where dripping fat was creating yet another flare-up.

Ten minutes later, it was definitely too late. She looked round to find three distinguished-looking

Japanese gentlemen watching her performance with apparent interest. Holly froze, at first, then remembered her manners and in a slightly dizzy state, managed to bow deeply to her audience.

All three men bowed equally deeply, and only then did the eldest approach and speak to her.

'That is ... a ... garden sprayer?' he asked, gesturing towards her pump-up sprayer. 'Surely you do not apply weed-spray to this?'

'No,' she chuckled. 'It's just water. To keep down the flare-ups. So the skin doesn't become charred.' And then had to demonstrate immediately just how the spray worked.

'Ah,' said the man. 'Very ingenious.' Whereupon all three approached more closely, drinks in hand, and stood there watching a much-bedraggled Holly as she supervised the final cooking of the pig.

It was only when Wade Bannister himself, obviously fresh from the shower, approached, that they broke off and moved forward to greet him. Leaving Holly only too aware of her grimy condition, but unable to do anything but turn her back on the whole affair.

That only lasted until a hand rested gently on her shoulder and a familiar voice rumbled in her ear. 'Are you enjoying this? Or is there some other reason for this ... rather unusual party gear?'

'Which would you rather have—tidy Holly and scorched pig or something fit for your guests to eat?' she muttered between gritted teeth, half inclined to turn the spray on Wade himself and walk off in a huff.

Obviously he'd returned late, and slipped through to his own room to shower and change into the casual but tidy blue denim outfit he now wore. His hair was still damp, and the denim clung to his body like a second skin, outlining the hard musculature, the erect bearing.

'I think I'd rather have a tidy Holly and properly

cooked pork,' he grinned, teeth gleaming against his tan. 'So I'll take over here, if you don't mind, while you run off and get cleaned up. But first—how's Jessica? I couldn't find her when I came in, and I didn't want to knock at the flat in case she's resting.'

'I imagine she's resting; I haven't seen her for nearly an hour,' Holly replied. 'But why don't you ask your hostess? I'm sure she knows everything that's relevant.'

Bitchy, she thought as she wound her way through the growing throng of guests, practically running in her bid to reach the privacy of the granny flat, but not angry enough to risk offending anyone.

Damn Wade Bannister anyway! How dare he just walk out of the bush like that, expecting everything to be done just right and not even think of the work that was involved? For just a moment, Holly thought of ignoring the rest of the party. She could quite happily curl up with a good book, or just go to sleep, for that matter. She was tired enough, after two days of Ramona Mason's commands and counter-commands and dithering.

Jessica's voice forestalled that particular desire.

'My goodness, look at you. Really, Holly, I thought you'd have gone and changed long ago. You haven't been out there looking like that with guests already here?'

'I have. And what's more, I don't care a fig,' Holly said in reply. 'In fact, I'm tempted to stay like this. No sense in getting all gussied up just so I can get filthy again when it comes time to carve that damned pig.'

'Wade will be carving the pig, I'm sure,' Jessica replied calmly, seeming to ignore Holly's fractious temper. 'Presuming he gets back in time, as I'm sure he will.'

'He's already back; couldn't you tell by the sound of Ramona cooing?' Now that, she realised, was totally bitchy, but for some reason, Holly just didn't care.

'He is? Well then, everything will be all right, won't it?' Jessica replied. 'So you whip into the shower and then put on something appropriate.' She, herself, was tidily dressed in a light hostess outfit that was both cool and stylish.

'Have we got a maid's uniform handy? That'd be just about appropriate,' Holly retorted, only to have her aunt reply: 'And try to do something about your temper, while you're at it. . This bitchiness doesn't become you, my dear.'

Neither, thought Holly, does being treated like a kitchen drudge, but I can see that's in store before this party's over. Still, I suppose there's nothing to be gained by falling in with dear Ramona's plans.

So when she emerged from the shower, feeling quite remarkably refreshed, Holly chose a light blouse and wrap-around skirt in pale green tones that highlighted her hair colour, and a pair of comfortable but stylish sandals to complete the outfit.

It wouldn't match Ramona's elegance, but at least she'd be comfortable, she thought.

The bulk of the guests had arrived in the interim, and Holly took some vague pleasure in the fact that most were dressed as casually as she and Wade. Ramona's outfit, while certainly elegant, was distinctly too formal for the tone of the party.

The blonde was playing the hostess role to the hilt, and Holly and Jessica, in silent agreement, left her to it. Jessica obviously knew many of their guests as friends, and Holly was quite content to busy herself making sure the canapés got round and that no one's glass was empty for too long.

As might have been expected, the rotating spit with its porky burden was the focal point of the party, and it wasn't long before Holly found herself holding an enormous serving tray as Wade slid heaping slices of

succulent pork on to it for distribution to the eagerly
waiting guests.

'You've done a marvellous job with this, Wade,' said
the first recipient, who in turn was a sort of celebrity as
the others watched that first, tantalising taste. 'Absolutely perfect.'

'Not my doing,' Wade replied easily. 'All the credit
for this little fat fellow belongs to Holly. I only came in
at the last minute to give her time to change.'

And Holly, both hands fully occupied in balancing
the huge tray, could only nod as guest after guest
expressed their pleasure. Her attempts to pass along the
credit to Jessica, who'd supervised the preparation of
the popular stuffing, went unnoticed by everyone but
Jessica herself, who toned down the compliment
considerably, and Wade, who grinned his own
acceptance of it. And Ramona, of course, whose
expression of scarce-contained fury left nothing to the
imagination.

When Holly had delivered the first platter to the row
of trestle tables and was about to return to have a
second one loaded, it was snatched from her fingers by
Ramona without a word.

Holly stood there, shaken by the violence and the
abruptness of the gesture, but after a moment she
relaxed and went in search of a drink for herself. What
did it matter, she thought, if Ramona found it necessary
to hog the limelight? Wade's compliment echoed in her
ears, and his smile came easily to memory. He'd been
pleased; nothing else mattered.

Inside of an hour, there was nothing left of the pig but a
few bones and infinitesimal bits of crackling that had
somehow been missed. 'I've never seen food disappear
like that in my entire life,' Holly muttered to Jessica as
they stood in a corner and watched. 'Did these people
starve themselves for days before coming, or what?'

'It was just enough,' Jessica replied as if she hadn't quite heard Holly's remark. 'There'll hardly be enough left for a pork sandwich for lunch tomorrow.'

'And just as well; I don't think I'd want to see such a thing in any event. It may be three weeks before I can face bacon and eggs, let alone roast pork,' Holly replied. In keeping with the guests, she'd done credit to her own work by eating what seemed to her to be an enormous amount, but had to admit that not only had she been hungry, but the roast pork *had* been very very good.

And now that the serious business of eating was done with, Wade's guests shifted to what seemed an equally serious business of partying. In the lounge room, the tape deck roared into life, the music conveyed to the patio by extension speakers and so loud that Holly hoped the neighbours were at the party. If not, she rather feared complaints.

People were dancing both inside the house and out, while those who weren't dancing were clustered in small groups from which erupted animated conversations.

Wade, needless to say, was being monopolised by Ramona, but Holly didn't concern herself with that. She drifted from group to group, occasionally allowing herself to be caught up in the dancing, occasionally hanging back to listen in on conversations so filled with technical jargon she could barely understand what they were about.

And she kept a weather-eye on Jessica, concerned that too much excitement might put a severe strain on her aunt. By ten o'clock, it was apparent that her concerns weren't totally without justification. Jessica approached Wade and a few minutes later advised Holly she was retiring.

'But not to worry. I feel fine, really I do. I haven't been overdoing things, and making a relatively early night of it is just a precaution. You stay on and enjoy yourself.'

Holly tried. She really, honestly tried. But with her aunt's departure, she found her attentions increasingly drawn to the mountains of dirty crockery and glassware that seemed to be growing in every corner.

'I don't fancy tomorrow,' she muttered to herself, and a moment later was surreptitiously involved in a campaign to get the dirty dishes out to the kitchen and at least sorted for the next day's clean-up campaign. There was a dishwasher, of course—Wade's home seemed to lack no single modern amenity. But the enormous amounts of crockery and cutlery would take three days to clean up using the dishwasher, so Holly chose instead to run through a load of glasses, just in case they were required yet that evening.

For the rest, it would be a long stint at the kitchen sink, and she was standing, drink in hand, contemplating that eventuality when she became aware of a new presence in the room.

'So this is where you've been hiding. You're a glutton for punishment, young Holly; this is no place to be during a party.'

Wade stood just inside the door, arms folded casually across his chest, his pale green eyes surveying Holly as she turned, startled, to meet his gaze.

'I ... I thought we might be needing more glasses, that's all,' she said, unaccountably aware that the music outside had changed, was now being played more softly and instead of being fast and vibrant it was slow, mellow. Waltz music, lovers' music.

'Uh-huh. And of course you weren't hiding or anything like that,' he said. Not making a question of it, except by the look in his eye.

'Of course not,' Holly replied. Why should she be hiding, after all? She'd done her part and more to make

the party a success, and any damned fool could see it
had been. Not that she'd be able to take much credit, of
course, because there'd be precious little left after
Ramona Mason claimed her giant's share. But hiding?
Not at all.

'Well, I'm glad of that, because there are several
people who wish to compliment you before they leave,
and I was afraid I'd have to tell them you'd gone off to
bed like some modern-day Cinderella,' Wade grinned,
taking her by the arm as he strode back towards the
lounge.

'As I thought. She was hiding in the kitchen,' he said
with a wider grin to the Japanese trio who'd been
among the first arrivals. Holly had spoken to them
during the party, and had even danced several times
with the youngest, but she was quite unprepared for the
sincerity of their compliments and their obvious
insistence on personally telling her how much they'd
enjoyed themselves.

Surely it should have been Ramona's place to receive
such comments, she thought, but was secretly pleased
with herself.

'Wade has promised us ... genuine bush barbecue,'
the youngest Japanese was saying. 'And when we
arrived, well, I thought this must be so. But now I think
he was perhaps joking with us. All ... much too
civilised to be proper bush barbecue.'

Holly was immediately aware of two things:
Ramona's spiteful glare from across the room, and
Wade's half-amused grin beside her. But there was little
she could reply to either circumstance.

'I'm only pleased you enjoyed it,' she replied
graciously, matching the Japanese deep, polite bows.
And would have taken leave of the situation right then,
except that Wade still held her by the arm, and kept
hold of her as he walked towards the front door with

his guests. There was nothing for it but to go with him and try to ignore the feeling of intimacy that the gesture conveyed.

The goodbyes said, he still didn't release her. Instead he escorted her back to where a few couples were drifting in a slow waltz, and without a word he turned Holly into his arms and stepped off to the music.

In his arms, she found herself transported. The warmth of his chest against hers, the light touch of his fingers against the small of her back, the subtle scent of him in her nostrils, all combined to make her shockingly aware of how vulnerable she became with this man. And how dangerous that could be for her.

With her eyes closed, it was even possible to ignore the mental daggers Ramona was throwing in her direction, although perhaps that was the cause of the tingling in her back, and not just Wade's exquisite touch.

But, she decided, it was simply too dangerous. Ramona had clearly staked her claim, and Wade, just as clearly, seemed to accept it. Any involvement he might have with Holly would be sheer dalliance, and she needed more than that. Much more.

When Wade made no attempt to release her after the third straight dance, Holly decided that she must take the initiative, while she still had the inner strength to do so. It would be only too easy to just keep dancing with him, to ignore the involvement of Ramona in his life, to ignore the danger signals her conscience kept flying as her body reacted to his touch.

'I'm really getting quite tired,' she said. 'Perhaps you should remember your hostly duties and spread yourself around a bit more.'

'If that's a subtle hint, I'd hate to see you when you're being straightforward,' he scowled. 'What's the matter—have I been treading on your toes?'

'Of course not; you're an excellent dancer.' As well you know, she thought. 'It's just that I am tired, and besides, I think I should look in on Aunt Jessica.'

'She looked fairly well rested,' Wade said, making no move to let her go. 'You must have done a pretty good job of keeping her from working too hard.'

'It wasn't nearly as difficult as I would have thought,' Holly said. 'I expected, well, you know her. But she was remarkably amenable, which worries me. I think she's a lot sicker than she's letting on.'

'So do I, but she's so damned proud and stubborn that she isn't going to give us any chance to help until it's very nearly too late. Have you tried talking to her about it?'

'Like talking to a brick wall,' Holly admitted. 'I really think you might do better; your opinion is very important to Jessica.'

'No more than yours, I'm sure,' he said, 'but I'll give it a go in the morning if you like. Because I think you're right; she's giving in too easily. Not like Jess; not at all.'

Whatever else he might have said was forestalled by the arrival of several party guests announcing their imminent departure, Ramona Mason hovering in their wake. Wade and Holly had barely stopped dancing and talking when the blonde interrupted.

'Darling,' she cried, 'Polly and Ian have just said they must take a cab home. At this time of night! Surely that isn't necessary. We could drive them, couldn't we?'

'Oh, don't bother yourself, Ramona,' said the man named Ian. 'We wouldn't think of putting you to such trouble. We only just stopped now to say good night and thank you; that's all.'

'It wouldn't be any trouble, mate,' Wade replied with an easy grin. 'I've not had enough to drink for that to be a problem, and to be honest I could use a bit of fresh air. Just give us a minute or two and we'll be off.'

'You're positive? I mean, really, it won't take that long to get a cab up here.'

'I'm absolutely positive,' Wade smiled. Then, surprisingly, reached out to snag Holly and draw her aside.

'You've said you're tired, so off to bed with you,' he hissed in her ear. 'We won't be long, I shouldn't think, but remember that if I find you in that kitchen, or even any evidence you've been there while I'm gone, there'll be trouble like you wouldn't believe. Understood?'

'Yes, massah,' she replied coldly. 'Whatever you say.'

'I say no dishwashing tonight,' was the calm reply. 'And none for darling Jessica, either. You've both done enough and more than enough today already.'

'Yesterday,' she replied automatically, then repeated herself at his quizzical glance. 'It's after midnight,' she finally explained.

'All the more reason for you to get to bed. I'd hate to have you turn into a pumpkin,' was the laughing reply. And he leaned down to brush a kiss across her forehead, then lightly smacked her behind, as if she was a ten-year-old being sent off to bed after dinner.

And with everybody watching! Holly didn't know whether to erupt with anger or hide her face with embarrassment, and by the time she might have made up her mind, it was already far too late; the front door was closing and she was alone.

'Damn,' she muttered aloud. 'Damn, damn, damn. The nerve of that arrogant so-and-so.' And she continued the diatribe as she flung herself around the patio and lounge room, tidying up the remaining empty glasses, emptying the ashtrays, doing all the usual things one does after a party.

She wouldn't oppose him by doing the dishes, nor would she be visible on his return at all, Holly decided. But it wasn't because of his masculine, chauvinistic authority; it was only that she couldn't bear to see him with Ramona Mason, much less be a witness to their sleeping arrangements on this particular night.

Fifteen minutes later, she lay silently in her own bed, stubbornly wishing for sleep to claim her before Wade's return. Stubbornly, but vainly. She was strung out, her emotions frazzled, her body tight with over-tiredness, her legs aching and her feet sore. But there was nothing the matter with her ears, which seemed perpetually pricked for the slightest sound to indicate Wade and Ramona's arrival.

She had checked on Jessica, who was sleeping soundly, and Holly found herself envying her aunt that ability. Especially when the drone of the returning motor car announced the start of a situation Holly couldn't bear even thinking about. She lay there, trying to force her ears not to hear.

'It was really quite a wonderful party, wasn't it, Wade, darling?' Ramona's voice, for some reason, penetrated even the drone of the air-conditioning. Almost, Holly couldn't help thinking, as if the blonde were deliberately pitching her voice to ensure that Holly might hear.

But I won't! I don't want to; I'm not interested, and I won't, Holly assured herself. Not that it helped.

The only consolation was that Wade's deep but softer-pitched tones carried much less. Only the occasional word drifted into comprehension from his replies.

'... pity your housekeeper wasn't well. She wasn't able to contribute very much at all. Her little niece did quite well, though, I thought, considering the circumstances.'

Condescending bitch, Holly thought, the spurt of anger overlying whatever reply Wade might have given.

'Bedtime? Yes, I suppose it is, darling. It must have been a very long day for you, and I'm quite exhausted after all the work ... going to come and tuck me ... ah, but of course, darling ...'

The rest was lost as they moved into the hallway between their rooms, fully across the house from where Holly lay gritting her teeth and trying both to hear and not to hear.

No prizes for guessing where Wade would spend the rest of his night, long day behind him or not, she thought. Which did nothing at all to help her get to sleep.

Holly lay there for nearly half an hour, then flung herself out of the bed and pulled on a loose towelling wrap. This was simply ridiculous! Worse, it was demeaning to be losing sleep over a man who couldn't care less.

Opening the door to her room, she peered down the darkened hallway, eyes and ears alert for any movement, any sound, But there was nothing.

Moving like a wraith, she eased through the lounge room, found the door to the hallway in Wade's section open, and silently closed it, then moved to the kitchen and closed that door as well.

With the air-conditioning going and all the doors shut, Holly was certain no sound could travel from the kitchen to where Wade and Ramona were either asleep or working up to it in ways she didn't care to contemplate. Well let them. She, regardless of Wade's earlier orders, was going to get stuck into the dishes.

'And to hell with you, Mr Wade Bannister,' she hissed beneath her breath. 'If I can't bloody well sleep, I might as well do something useful, and if you don't like it, you can jolly well stick it up your jumper!'

Half an hour later, she was wishing she'd waited until morning to begin the chore. Once begun, she felt compelled to finish the job., but despite having gone through three sink loads of soapy water and dishes, she barely seemed to be making any headway at all. It might have helped if she'd used the dishwasher for the glasses, but she was afraid its rumbling vibrations might carry through the house.

Worse, she'd run the fourth sink too hot, which necessitated taking a break until it had cooled down sufficiently for her to continue. She'd worn through the fingers of the last pair of rubber gloves in the kitchen, and didn't dare reach in to try and release some of the water with her bare fingers.

'To hell with it; I'll have a cup of coffee and see if that smartens me up,' she muttered under her breath. Then, having got the jug boiled, she decided hot chocolate might be a wiser choice, and began mixing that, instead.

She was just stirring the brew when Wade's voice intruded, an angry growl that sent the cup flying from suddenly nerveless fingers to crash upside down on the kitchen table.

CHAPTER SIX

HOLLY flew to her feet, but he was there before her, the kitchen sponge in hand and tea-towel following it as he caught the spilled liquid before it could pour down on to the carpet.

'Are you always this clumsy?' he asked, voice now strangely soft after the growling enquiry that had so startled her.

'Only when people sneak up on me and start growling,' Holly retorted, grabbing away the tea-towel and rushing over to wring it into the still-full sink. Oh . . . now look what you've made me do.'

'I doubt that it'll cause much of a problem,' he replied, dunking the sponge into the soapy water and then yanking back his fingers with a yelp of surprise. 'What the hell? Are you determined to scald yourself as well?'

'Obviously not. That's why I was having a drink, to give that time to cool,' she replied.

'Well, you can make me one, too,' he said, shaking his hand as if to ease the pain. 'Damn, but that was hot. You might have warned me.'

'You hardly gave me a chance, did you?' Holly snapped. 'And if you want a drink, make your own. What are you doing, sneaking around like some sort of spook in the night?'

'Hardly sneaking.' His voice softened. 'And besides, it is my house. I do live here, in case you'd forgotten.'

'How could I possibly?' she scoffed, forgetting her earlier determination as she spooned hot chocolate into two fresh cups. 'That doesn't explain what you're doing in the kitchen; I would have thought you'd be . . .' And she broke off, suddenly aware of what she'd nearly said.

'And just where did you think I'd be?' he asked, his eyes narrowing in wicked speculation. 'Well . . . aren't you game to say it? It's not as if I couldn't figure out what you meant, after all.'

'If you're so smart at figuring things out, then you hardly need to be told,' she responded, avoiding his eyes as she continued mixing their drinks. 'The point is, you oughtn't to be here, and you certainly shouldn't have snuck up on me like that. I . . . well . . . I might have screamed and wakened the entire house.'

'Which certainly would have been interesting,' he said, reaching out to take one cup from her. 'You might stop that stirring now, unless you're bound and determined to wear the bottom out of the cup.' Taking the cup, he moved silently over to sit down at the end of the table, gesturing to Holly to sit herself across from him.

It was only at that instant she realised he was still completely dressed, still wearing the same denim shirt and trousers he'd had on during the party. And it was only at that instant she realised that *she* wasn't fully dressed, but had only the towelling robe, loosely closing at the best of times, between herself and Wade Bannister's probing eyes.

'That's quite an outfit for doing dishes in,' he grinned, wickedly, deliberately cruising with his eyes along the loose opening of the robe. 'But then of course, you didn't expect to be disturbed, did you? You thought I was, shall we say, otherwise occupied?'

'Certainly a reasonable assumption,' Holly said. 'At any rate, I certainly didn't expect to be disturbed. And I wish I hadn't been; you quite startled me.'

'Only fair, I'd say, considering you're breaking your promise to me. Or have you got some perfectly valid reason to be out here in the small hours of the morning doing dishes after having promised you wouldn't?'

'Why should it matter? They've got to be done sooner or later, and I, well, I felt like doing them now.'

'Because you couldn't sleep? I find that hard to believe, considering the day you must have put in. By rights, you should be dead on your feet, not standing up to the sink and facing what amounts to another day's work.'

Holly shrugged. 'At least this way I can sleep comfortably, knowing I shan't have to face them when I do get up.'

Wade sipped at his hot chocolate, eyeing her silently across the length of the table. 'And of course it wouldn't have a thing to do with the fact that if they're done by morning, dear Jessica won't have a chance to start on them before there's anyone up and about to stop her?'

'What a wonderful excuse; I wish I'd thought of it,' Holly replied with a sudden grin. 'But no, that never entered my mind. I just ... couldn't sleep so I thought I'd make a start on them. Simple as that.'

Wade's smile wasn't sudden. Nor was it really a smile, Holly realised, seeing in his eyes the beginning of something that might be emerging anger. 'And I suppose it never entered your mind either that I might be serious when I specified disposables for this party,' he said grimly. And before Holly could reply, 'I wasn't only thinking of Jessica, you know? I was trying to ensure that this sort of thing didn't happen—didn't *have* to happen.'

'I ... well ...' She didn't know what to say, short of a straight-out placement of blame on Ramona, where it belonged. Wade didn't give her that chance.

'And of course it never entered your mind that I might be damned angry—and justifiably angry—at

having my orders so blatantly countermanded? Or did
you even bother to think about that?'

'Considering it wasn't me who made the decision, no,
I didn't,' Holly retorted. Angry, now, she continued
over his attempt to interrupt. 'All of which is something
you could have found out quite easily, without getting
up in the middle of the night to harangue me about it, I
might add.'

'Ah,' he said, 'so you didn't make the decision, eh?
Well then tell me, dear Holly, just how many women
there are in my house with distinctly English accents?
And how many of those, pray tell, might have
telephoned to order all this, this damned crockery? Tell
me that?'

'I can only tell you that it wasn't me,' Holly replied,
her mind spinning at the implications of what he'd said.
She ran the circumstances of the past few days through
a mental replay, but found it impossible to determine if
she'd actually been in the room when Ramona had
taken charge of ordering up the glassware, crockery and
silverware.

'I see.' But he didn't; she could tell that by the velvet-
iron tone in his voice. And he didn't believe her, either.
'Well, if you didn't order all this stuff, and if you didn't
deliberately countermand my orders, then why are you
out here in the middle of the night washing up?'

'What?' Holly couldn't find the logic in that question
at all. 'I'm washing up because *somebody*'s got to do it,'
she finally added after a moment's silence in which
Wade only stared at her. 'And since we've already
agreed that Jessica shouldn't be doing it, and since I
can't imagine *you* doing it, that leaves me.'

'Oh,' he said, and there was something now in his
eyes besides accusing anger. 'So you can't imagine *me*
doing it. Now I wonder why that is. Am I supposedly
so helpless just because I'm a man, or have I impressed

you somehow as a ruthless, heartless employer who'd expect Jess to rise out of her sick-bed to clean up?'

'Stop being silly,' Holly retorted even before she'd thought.

'What's silly about it? Do you really think I'm afraid of a bit of soap and water, young Holly? Because if you do, then you're in for a surprise,' Wade snarled, then gulped down the remainder of his hot chocolate—now lukewarm chocolate—and rose lithely to his feet.

'Since you're such a disbeliever, you can dry,' he muttered. 'That's the part I like least, anyway.'

And before she could even get up, he was elbow-deep in the sink, wincing only slightly as his hands encountered the still-too-hot dishwater.

'Well, don't just sit there, pick up a tea-towel and get at it,' he shot back over his shoulder. 'There are plenty of better ways of spending the night with a woman dressed as you are, so let's not dilly-dally around here in the kitchen.'

'If you're going to be like that about it, I think I'll just go and change, first,' Holly replied, bemused by his attitude, but none the less only too conscious of her attire.

'Suit yourself, but I'd suggest you be quick about it,' Wade replied, not even bothering to look at her. 'This stuff is going to be washed, dried, packed away and ready to go before either of us gets any sleep, and that's an order you damned well *will* obey.'

'I'm not sure I will,' Holly replied with a sudden grin that Wade couldn't see. 'Maybe I'll just lock myself in my room and leave you to it.'

It was the wrong thing to have said; Holly realised that immediately when he crossed the room in two huge strides, soapy hands clamping about her waist so tightly she could hardly breathe.

'If that's your attitude, then you'll just have to help

out dressed as you are,' he said, staring down at her as if from a great height. 'Not that it'll make things any easier, because I may have trouble keeping my mind on my work, but it'll certainly set the scene for afterwards, once the work's done and the fun can begin, won't it?'

His eyes dropped from her own to the gaping neckline of the robe, then one hand lifted from her waist to run a swift caress across her breast before deftly twitching the robe taut. Holly felt her nipple swell immediately, responding with Pavlovian certainty to his touch.

'Or maybe we could just leave the dishes for now,' he said, voice soft in her ear just before his lips touched the lobe in a light, thistle-down kiss.

'Or maybe you could just put your hands back in the sink where they belong,' Holly snapped, putting both hands against his chest and shoving him away with an ease she immediately knew was only because he'd allowed it. Surprisingly, he obeyed, and when she moved in beside him, tea-towel in hand, she found herself wondering why. Had he indeed come to the kitchen from Ramona's bed, as she'd first thought?

Holly found herself, ludicrously, attempting to sort out the scent of Ramona's perfume from the heady aroma of the dish soap, her own perfume and Wade's own, personal and highly distinctive aroma, tangy and distinctly masculine.

Surely if he had ... well ... there would be some evidence, she found herself thinking. Or would there?

'Stop thinking and start drying,' said a dry voice to her right. 'The best thing about doing dishes is that you shouldn't have to think.'

Holly looked down to find that she'd been just standing there, dish-towel in hand, for ... how long? Long enough for Wade to have got ahead of her, and now he lounged easily against the edge of the sink, watching with sardonic amusement as she rushed to catch up.

'I'm sorry,' she murmured, speeding up her movements and wishing he'd look somewhere else, at somebody, something else, and not just amuse himself by surveying every movement of her scantily clad figure.

For the next half-hour, they worked silently, side-by-side and yet as if they were divided by some invisible barrier. Wade now seemed less angry, but submerged in his own mind, his strong fingers sliding through the routine without any evidence of conscious thought.

Holly, by comparison, might have looked as if she was doing the same, but in fact she was becoming increasingly sensitised to his presence beside her in a situation that was strangely domestic, uniquely comfortable.

Then, almost without warning, it was finished. The final handful of cutlery emerged from the sink, the dingy soap-suds disappeared in a gurgle that seemed loud in the silence of the room, and Wade was stepping away from the sink.

'I'll start packing now,' he said simply, and without any further gesture, proceeded to do just that. Holly finished off her drying, then silently began to help him, and again they worked without speaking until all the rented utensils were stowed away and ready to be returned.

Wade stood there for a moment afterwards, noticeably swaying for a second before he shook his head in extreme weariness. 'There. That's done, thank God,' he muttered, then turned to Holly. 'And whatever else they say about us, we'll make marvellous housewives someday, my girl, at least in the kitchen. Do you think you'll be able to sleep now—now that all this is out of the way?'

Holly, stricken by the tiredness in his face, by the deep lines and the sunken eyes, answered with a question of her own. 'Never mind me. How long is it since you've slept? You look as if it's been days.'

'Has been,' he replied. 'This is ... what ... Saturday morning? Feels like a Monday morning, but then ... well ... I had a good sleep on Wednesday night, I think it was.'

'You ... you're mad. Quite mad,' Holly raged. 'Going without sleep that long and then having the nerve, the utter stupidity, to stand up here all night and wash dishes!'

'Like somebody said, they had to be done,' he replied with a slow, gentle grin. 'I rather enjoyed it, actually. Helped me to relax, which I usually have trouble doing after a party. Sometimes I don't know why I have parties at all; I invariably have this kind of reaction.'

'So what was your excuse on Thursday night?' Holly found herself demanding, immediately aware that it was absolutely none of her business, and yet ...

'Driving,' he replied simply. 'Thursday, Thursday night and all day Friday.'

'From Marble Bar? That's not a two-day trip, surely.'

'It is the way I came,' Wade replied wearily. 'I had things to do in Newman and Mount Tom Price and Yarraloola on the way, which sort of complicated the route a bit.'

'Things that were so important you couldn't even stop and sleep? Or is life out here so much in the fast-lane that people are expected to go without indefinitely?' Holly snorted, knowing she must sound like a fishwife, but unable to halt the truly astonished anger she felt.

'Sometimes it gets a bit hectic, is all,' Wade replied stifling a yawn to do it. 'And I didn't go entirely without sleep; I managed to catnap here and there along the way.'

'Probably while you were driving,' she replied. 'And then you've got the nerve to criticise me for staying up to do a few dishes.'

'Certainly. I'm used to it, for one thing. You're not; and what's more, you've barely had time to get acclimatised. I'll have five hours sleep and be back to normal, but you, young Holly, will sleep the clock around. Just wait and see.'

'That is the most ridiculous thing I've ever heard,' Holly cried. 'It isn't me who's standing there swaying like a drunken sailor, and it isn't me who's obviously dead on their feet.'

'And it wouldn't be Wade, either, if you'd stop harping at him,' said a new voice, and both of them turned to see Jessica standing just inside the doorway. Wrapped in an old towelling gown, she shook her head in obvious exasperation as she surveyed first one, then the other. Then she looked at the stacks of rental cutlery and crockery.

'You're both mad. You're as bad as each other,' Jessica muttered. Clearly, she'd had a relatively good night, having slept from ten o'clock until—Holly realised—almost six. 'Here you are, screaming at each other like a couple of stray cats about something neither of you can change, and without enough sense between you to go to bed—where you both damned well belong.'

Both of them stared at her, astonished by the outburst, but it was Wade who recovered first.

'What are you doing up at this ungodly hour?' he demanded, quite ignoring Jessica's indignation. 'I suppose you thought you'd steal a march on Holly by getting stuck into these dishes while we were all asleep?'

'I am up,' Jessica replied firmly, 'because I've had enough sleep, and because the noise you two have been making for the past few minutes would wake almost anyone. As for the dishes, it wouldn't have hurt me to make a start on them, although since it was your friend Ramona who insisted on having them in the first place, I would have thought it perhaps fair if she'd at least helped to wash up.'

'And I was going to, of course, but surely it could have waited until a more civilised hour,' said yet another voice, and Ramona strode into the room, her slender body wrapped in a pegnoir so sheer it was almost indecent, her long blonde hair only slightly rumpled from sleep.

'Goodness,' she sighed, putting one hand up to cover a yawn. Her eyes strayed across the neatly stacked party equipment and then to the three figures who stood staring at her in honest surprise. 'Is this what all the racket's been about? Have you two been here *all* night, doing *this*?'

Nobody replied, and Ramona shook her head distractedly. 'Mad, you're quite mad,' she sighed. 'I . . . I don't understand any of this; I'm going back to bed.'

'What a splendid idea; I wish I'd thought of it,' Wade muttered in a sarcastic voice, with an equally sarcastic glare at Holly. Then he walked out, practically on Ramona's heels.

Holly said nothing as Jessica gently steered her into her own bedroom, pointed significantly towards the bed, then left without another word.

Half-determined not to sleep, Holly threw herself on to the bed and picked up a book she'd been reading. It was still on her lap when she woke with a start and immediately looked to the bedside clock.

Five o'clock! She was congratulating herself when a glance out the window told her unmistakably that it was five o'clock in the morning and that she had, just as that damned Wade Bannister had predicted, slept the clock around.

Hardly daring to believe it, Holly rushed through her toilet, threw on a pair of shorts and a top, then hurried to the kitchen as quickly as she could without making her haste obvious.

'Hi there, sleeping beauty. Ready for some breakfast?'

And no mistaking the smugness, the unholy gleam of laughter in those pale green eyes. Her immediate retort—'You didn't beat me by much'—died unspoken as she looked round to find that all the rental equipment was gone and that Wade was obviously the person who'd returned it. Which meant he must have been up and mobile sometime during the day before.

'I think perhaps just some coffee. I'll get it,' she finally managed to say, unwilling to meet the challenge in his eyes.

'You'll have breakfast, although if you really can't bear my company you can wait and have it with Jessica,' was the grinning reply. 'And don't say you're not hungry, because it just wouldn't be believable considering how long you've been asleep.'

'Doesn't it bother you sometimes to be such a know-it-all?' Holly replied ruefully as she poured a cup of coffee and then, defiantly, walked over to sit down across the table from Wade. 'Obviously not as much as it bothers you,' he replied carelessly. 'I see that a good long rest hasn't done anything for your disposition, not that I expected it to.'

'There's nothing wrong with my disposition except that it doesn't like being picked on first thing in the morning,' Holly retorted. 'You, of course, have no such problem. I'm sure you had your five hours of sleep, worked a full day, made all sorts of money, or progress, or whatever it is you do, and then went to bed at midnight last night to have another five hours of sleep.'

'Oh, stop being so bitchy,' he replied with less than

his earlier cheerfulness. 'If it's any consolation, I slept until two o'clock yesterday afternoon, got the rental stuff returned, put Ramona on the plane to Perth, and then slept from four o'clock until about fifteen minutes ago, which doesn't put me very much ahead of you.'

What to say to that? Holly could think of nothing, so she concentrated her attention on her coffee cup, wishing that maybe, someday, she'd learn to keep her mouth shut. The two of them were still embraced in a rather strained silence when Jessica entered the room.

She stood there for a moment, looking from one to the other as they offered good mornings, then replied with a wry grin. 'Well I suppose it's an improvement over yesterday's slanging match, but you'll have to do better than this if I'm to feel comfortable leaving the two of you alone tomorrow,' she said.

Holly was at first startled, then remembered that Jess had indeed made arrangements to return to Perth the next day for her final tests. Wade merely growled into his coffee cup, now empty, and rose to get himself a refill. They were all at the table before he finally spoke.

'We're not going to be alone,' he said. 'I think Holly ought to go with you.'

Holly's 'Oh, yes,' and Jessica's quieter but far more determined 'No!' collided in mid-air, and Wade caught his cue with astonishing dexterity.

'Which gives me the casting vote, I think,' he said with a satisfied grin. 'And I say she goes.'

'Too bad.' Jessica's mouth had firmed and her eyes blazed with determination. 'Because I say she stays. You know very well that I'll be away perhaps as long as a week, and you just cannot take that long away from your field trips at this time. Also, and please, Holly, don't be upset by this, but I really would prefer to handle this alone. Having you along would not be the comforting factor we'd both like; it would only upset me because you'd be worrying.'

'Ignoring, of course, the fact that we'd both be worrying here,' Wade growled before Holly could speak. 'Damn it, Jess, there's no reason at all why Holly shouldn't go, except for your damned stubbornness.'

'There is every reason. I am going to be under strain enough without having to worry about what's happening here,' Jessica replied without turning a hair. 'So if you're really as concerned as you profess to be, you will please, *please* just do as I ask. I'll be much happier knowing everything here is under control. Now please let's drop this discussion. I know that both of you have the best of intentions, but I want Holly to stay here and that's that!'

Holly herself was about to interject, but the rising colour in her aunt's face and Wade's barely perceptible gesture of warning stopped her. It was left for him to acquiesce for both of them, and he did it not too grudgingly.

'All right, have it your own way,' he agreed. 'Provided I get regular progress reports and you promise to behave.'

'Agreed,' said Jessica, and immediately changed the subject so that they spent breakfast discussing Wade's general travel plans for the coming week. After the meal, he disappeared into the garage, where he spent the entire day servicing the truck he used for bush travel. Holly and Jessica tidied the house, doing last-minute laundry and packing but not—as if by tacit agreement—discussing the upcoming tests or Holly's futile wish to accompany Jessica.

At dinner that night, all three were quieter than usual, and they all went to bed earlier than usual in preparation for Jess's early-morning departure. In the morning, the quietness was exchanged for a more

cheerful, companionable attitude, but it was a slightly
forced cheerfulness that none of them really tried to push.

It was only after they'd waved away Jessica's plane
that Wade relaxed his temper enough to show Holly
how deeply he felt about the whole circumstance
created by her aunt's independence.

'I'm going to have to leave this to you,' he said as the
plane disappeared into the incredible blue of the Pilbara
sky. 'If you like, we'll have you on the next plane, and
once you're on the spot, I doubt if there's much Jess
will be able to do about it.'

'Except fret and get all upset,' Holly replied after a
long silence in which she thought about Wade's
incredible proposal. 'And she would. Lord, but I've
never seen such infernal independence. No, I guess I'd
better do as she says and stay here.'

'You wouldn't have to let her know you were there,'
he mused. 'And at least then you'd be close at hand,
just in case.'

'And what happens when she telephones at some
ungodly hour and I'm not here? I don't think she'd
accept your excuses.'

'There wouldn't be any, because I hadn't intended to
be here,' he replied. 'But of course that would only add
to her worries, wouldn't it? Damn the woman! I'm
sorry, Holly, because I understand how much you'd
prefer to be with her, but I just can't see a way to
manage it.'

'Neither can I, so we'll just have to string along with
her wishes. For now, anyway. I gather from what you
just said that you're planning another trip away.'

'Soon as I get you home,' he replied. 'But it won't be
a long one; I should be back tomorrow night or the day
after, sometime. You'll be okay?'

'Of course,' she replied. 'I can worry here just as
easily as in Perth, as Jessica said.'

'Well try not to; I've already made sure she's in the best possible hands, and I'll be leaving you some phone numbers, in case she decides to get sneaky and not tell you everything she should. If I'm delayed for any reason, you'll be able to get the information first-hand.'

Once they were home, Wade lost no time in loading up his vehicle and getting ready for the journey. He left Holly with a list of phone numbers, far more money than she could imagine ever needing, and instructions on how and where to charge most of the things she might need.

'You're taking a chance there,' she said. 'I could easily leave you with a stack of bills and a ruined credit rating.'

'Don't be ridiculous,' he retorted, anger shivering behind his eyes for just an instant. Then he advised her to go off and play at being a tourist, leapt into his vehicle, and was away without even a proper farewell. No touch, no kiss, no gentleness, except for an unfathomable glance and the hint of a departing smile. Holly didn't know if she'd wanted him to kiss her goodbye or not, but she missed the gesture.

It almost seemed, Holly thought after he'd gone, as if Wade's attempts to have her accompany Jessica were more because he didn't want her in his house—or alone with him?—than because of her own wish to be with Jess. And yet why should he feel that way? Not, surely, because of that ridiculous incident in the Perth airport?

And certainly it wasn't because he feared her trying to seduce him—if anything it would be the other way round. Not that she considered that a problem; Wade Bannister was most unlikely to force his attentions upon her without some encouragement, and that was something he just mustn't have. It was simple as that.

Except—she knew that she really didn't feel much like being alone. Not now, not with Jessica's stubbornness and unresolved tests hanging like an albatross on her mind.

But what else to do—except perhaps take Wade's advice and play tourist for the rest of the day? Which didn't really appeal either. Tomorrow she might take his advice, but not today.

So she stayed at home, wrote several long overdue letters to friends in England, idly wished there was some housework left to be done, and found time going from tedious to boring to horribly boring as she began to experience for the first time the true isolation and loneliness that Port Hedland could offer.

In the evening, she went for a long walk, then tried to concentrate on television while she waited for Jessica to phone an all too brief call, and tried to keep her mind from being too aware of the absent Wade Bannister.

Next morning, she arose far too early; although the relative coolness of the dawn air was pleasant, there was simply nothing to do but some over-cautious sunbathing until the rest of the community awoke. Then, she devoted herself to the role of tourist, and did it with a vengeance spurred on by Wade having suggested that in the first place.

Holly managed, with surprisingly little difficulty, to drive every single road and street in the community by early afternoon. And that was religiously following the tourist guide map she appropriated as soon as the tourist bureau had opened for the day.

It was, she supposed, a fascinating place. At least, it should have been. But the fascination was overshadowed by the raw newness, the haunting aura of impermanence. She was unable to tour the most logical attraction, the Mount Newman Mining Company's port facility, for one of the most logical reasons. Everybody was on strike, a situation Jessica had mentioned as being almost as common as having the men working. But

Holly made up for that questionable lack by driving through the town's general port area, feeling somewhat overwhelmed by the immense ore carriers, the mountain of iron ore and the vigorous town activity that denied the growing heat of the day.

In tonnage terms, she discovered, it was the largest port in Australia, taking millions of tonnes each year on to ships so large they defied description.

She spent some time wandering across the edges of the tidal inlet called 'Pretty Pool', described as a haven for shell collectors. But she found it was also a haven for sandflies, and cut her visit short. She was also unable to free her imagination from the display of hostile stonefish and sea snakes she'd viewed at the tourist bureau.

It was vaguely annoying, she decided, to find evidence of marvellous seaside facilities that became virtually unusable for so much of the year because of the deadly sea snakes and the ever-constant danger of treading upon a stone-fish.

The stone-fish, she thought, must be the ugliest marine creature in existence, a prehistoric creature still somehow existing in the modern world because of the same poisonous nature that had kept it alive centuries before. She resolved never, ever, to set foot on the reefs without the stoutest of footwear.

A far more interesting attraction was the Kingsmill Street headquarters of the Royal Flying Doctor service, the world-renowed life-line between the far-flung outback areas of Australia and the isolated centres that served them. Holly listened in fascination to the scheduled radio 'galah session' in which all the outlying properites used the radio network like a telephone in a fast-moving gossip and information exchange whose casualness belied the serious importance of the service.

Was Wade out there somewhere, she wondered,

linked to her unknowingly by this invisible chain of faceless voices, each one its own bastion against the loneliness of the next?

And later, as her drive to view the shimmering wasteland of the salt company's evaporation ponds beside the North West Coastal Highway revealed more of the sheer vastness of the country, the flat, bleak, yet somehow still-beautiful emptiness, she wondered how any so-called civilised man could have withstood the emptiness to settle and survive here.

And how the original inhabitants, the naked and nomadic Aborigines, could have survived was beyond wonder—especially for a girl who could get sunburned even in the shade! Holly shuddered and resolved to investigate Wade's extensive library for more information before she tried to reach any conclusions on that particular subject.

As the afternoon heat made even driving uncomfortable, she devoted herself to touring a private collection of sea-shells and Aboriginal artifacts, and another of local handicrafts, then steered for the surprisingly large and well-serviced shopping centre in South Hedland.

It was fully air-conditioned, almost too much so, she thought, marvelling at the broad racial and cultural mix that was obvious to even the most casual observer. Local Aborigines mingled with colourfully dressed, soft-spoken Malaysians and families of every conceivable European background, to judge from the accents she heard.

And there was money. A good deal of it, to judge from the high-heaped shopping carts and the range of pure luxury items that seemed incredibly extensive for such a small community.

Roughly fifteen thousand people, almost all of them totally dependent upon the mining industry for their livelihood, she realised. And yet despite the relative isolation they seemed to lack no tangible evidence of a fully modern, typical consumer lifestyle.

Almost every item in every aspect of living was top-of-the-line or close to it. The prices were, to Holly's inexperienced eye, astronomically high. But there was certainly no lack of customers. The reason, at least in part, was revealed when she paused for a cool drink and a sandwich and overheard the conversation between two women at the next table.

'I worry a bit about the kids, sometimes,' one was saying. 'It seems there just isn't anything they want that we can't afford to buy for them—and Bill does buy it, never fear. It just can't be healthy, and yet, what else is there? We can't afford to leave even if we wanted to, not for another few years. And there's so little for kids, really.'

'I don't think we'll ever be able to leave,' her companion replied. 'And for the same reason—we spend it as fast as we make it. But, they're things we couldn't afford anywhere else, and Geoff likes his work, so why worry? I can stick it out for another few years, anyway, and then we'll see.'

The two women left shortly, but Holly lingered, eavesdropping shamelessly on whatever other conversations were in a form of English she could understand. It was enlightening.

Some people loved the place; some hated it. But without exception the people she overheard regarded the town as only a temporary aspect of their lives. All had families somewhere else, interests somewhere else, and considered Port Hedland a means to an end, a place to make the money to get out of.

The town, certainly, wasn't temporary. Given, at least, reasonable consideration from cyclones and world iron prices, it was here to stay. But would it always, she wondered, have that somewhat tragic air of human impermanence? Or would there be, one day, an entire breed of Northwesters like Wade, who obviously felt none of this transient, fleeting temporariness she found in almost everyone else?

It was difficult to judge, especially from the viewpoint of a visitor whose own permanence was, to say the least, rather questionable. And could she ever consider herself living so far from everything she'd grown up with, far from the theatre, the arts, the incredibly ancient—by Port Hedland standards—history of her own country?

Jessica had managed, but at what personal price? She recalled hearing her aunt say that the town's second-biggest industry must be that of video recorders and video movies which were rented at quite inexpensive rates. A large percentage of the town's population had them, Holly had been told, renting movies often every night of the week.

Wade had mentioned at one point that he had seriously thought of putting in a swimming pool, but he feared the amount of extra work it would entail, especially during cyclone times, and the fact that he didn't think Jessica would use it often enough to justify the expense and the desecration of the garden that would be involved.

It wasn't until later that evening, long after the tropical sun had performed its daily magic trick of disappearing into the sea almost instantaneously, that Holly realised how often that day she'd given half-serious consideration to staying in the Northwest permanently.

'I must be mad!' she exclaimed aloud at the sudden realisation. Then looked self-consciously over her shoulder as if expecting somebody—Wade, perhaps?—to be observing her. It was thought-provoking to admit that it was *his* influence and little else that had created such considerations.

Would he be back the next day? Or perhaps yet tonight? And when he arrived, would he still be so cold, so determined to shut her out of every aspect of life except Jessica?

Jessica, who hadn't yet telephoned that evening. And who should have, Holly realised. Certainly she wouldn't be leaving it until nearly midnight?

Holly found the telephone number for the flat, almost completed dialling it, then abruptly hung up. It was also too late for her to be ringing. What if Jessica was asleep, exhausted from her tests? She might just have forgotten, and would surely ring in the morning. If not, well Wade should be back and would surely know what to do.

None of these thoughts made it easier for Holly to sleep. She was restless, edgy, awake every few hours wondering if Wade had returned and if Jessica was all right. Morning took forever to arrive.

With the first rays of morning sun, Holly was sitting at the kitchen table, already into her third cup of coffee and wondering how early she dared telephone the flat in Perth. Certainly, she thought, not quite *this* early.

But at seven o'clock she could wait no longer, and dialled the number with fingers shaking from an over-abundance of coffee in her system. It rang, rang some more, and finally rang off, leaving her no wiser than before. Could Jessica have slept through that? Or was there some device for turning off the telephone bell, or did Jessica have the phone locked away in a cabinet, as Wade had once done?

She tried again half an hour later, and again at eight o'clock, but the result was the same. Then she became really worried and started ringing the other numbers Wade had left her, only to find a series of recordings advising her to try again after nine.

But when she finally did get through, at one minute

past nine, it was only to be told that the doctor could tell her nothing, and indeed *would* tell her nothing. 'Just have Mr Bannister ring us, preferably as soon as possible,' the woman at the other end of the telephone insisted. And hung up over Holly's protests that *she* was Jessica's blood relative, not Mr Wade Bannister.

When Wade himself walked in ten minutes later, almost unrecognisable through a coating of reddish-pink Pilbara dust, his grin faded before the fury that Holly unleashed before he'd even got through the door.

CHAPTER SEVEN

'SETTLE down, damn it,' Wade shouted just as Holly was getting fully wound up, her verbal assault screaming into top gear and her body ready to launch a physical attack to match.

'Settle down? How the hell can you *dare* to tell me that?' she squalled. She was half crouched, her hands extended, nails ready to claw out at him in her fierce anger. 'You ... you utter bastard! How dare you arrnage it so the doctors wouldn't tell me what's happening? Jessica is *my* aunt; *I'm* her only blood kin, but they want to talk to *you*. Why you? What possible right can you have to ...'

'Damn it, I've probably got nearly as much as you have,' he snarled. 'But that isn't the point. The point is that I didn't arrange any such thing! Did NOT! Have you got that? I don't have the faintest idea what's going on, except maybe that somebody's screwed up in Perth, but if you'll just settle down and act like a civilised person, and let me get on the telephone, then we'll both know.'

'But ...' She got no further. Hands like iron clamps shot out to grip her shoulders, and then she was being shaken until her teeth rattled.

'But—nothing!' And she was flung halfway across the room, her bottom landing in a chair with a resounding, thoroughly sobering thud.

'Now sit down, shut up, and maybe in a minute we'll have this straightened out,' Wade growled. 'And don't even think about getting up, or interrupting me, unless you want that pretty little backside tanned for you. Is that clear?'

He didn't wait for a reply; didn't so much as glance to see if she'd heard. Already he was lifting the telephone receiver, dialling the appropriate number with fingers that trembled with his anger.

He spoke for perhaps three minutes, then shook a finger at Holly to keep her immobile and made yet another call. That one took only slightly longer, and from Wade's portion of the conversation, Holly found herself prepared to believe the worst.

'Damn Jessica anyway,' he cursed when he'd hung up after the second call. 'When this is over, I'll have her head on a plate, mark my very words. And you should, too, because she's the reason you couldn't get any information. Bloody stupid woman!'

'What? Jessica is the reason? But ... but ...' Holly was floundering, her brain incapable of assimilating his comments.

'Yes. Jessica! Your dear, beloved aunt and my addle-brained housekeeper,' Wade retorted. 'She didn't want to worry you, or maybe she just realised you might go all to pieces. How the hell do I know? Anyway, she specifically organised things so that they wouldn't tell anybody but me.'

'Tell you what? What? That's what I want to know,' Holly cried.

'Tell me—us—that she's been lying like a bloody footpath all along,' Wade raged. 'This second run of tests wasn't tests at all—the damned woman's in there having surgery today. That's what she doing.'

'Surgery? Oh, surely she wouldn't ...' Holly paused, only too aware that Jessica would, could, and obviously had. Wade's face told her that. No question about it.

'And people wonder why there are male chauvinists,' he muttered disgustedly. 'Lord love us, the things some women will do.' Then he sobered considerably. 'Yes, surgery. Not, apparently, the most serious surgery one might imagine, but serious enough that it'll be this evening before we'll know if it's gone successfully.'

'And what are we supposed to do in the meantime— sit here biting our nails?' Holly asked, not bothering to hide the bitterness she felt. Damn her aunt for being so stubbornly independent!

'Not bloody likely,' Wade replied, a new determination in his eyes. 'I'm going to start by having a shower and shave; and if you'd like to change into your swimsuit and put something over it, we'll get the hell out of here and see if we can't find some lunch.'

'Lunch? But it's barely nine o'clock in the morning,' Holly argued. Wade was already leaving the room, moving towards the laundry so smoothly that what dust remained on his work clothes seemed held to them by static electricity.

'Okay, then we'll have coffee first,' he replied over his shoulder. 'I just want to get out of this gear before we end up with half the Pilbara in here.'

A few minutes later, the coffee just poured and Holly still unsure of his plans, he re-entered the room, this time dressed in fresh jeans and a light denim shirt, busily scrubbing at his hair with a towel.

'I hope you've not had a mammoth breakfast,' he grinned. 'Where we're going for lunch, you'll need all the appetite you can muster.' Then he disappeared again, only to emerge a moment later with his hair combed and his feet in light leather sandals.

'So, what have you been doing with yourself while I've been gone—apart from worrying about Jessica?' he asked, sitting down and reaching for his coffee in a gesture so domestic it made Holly's heart lurch.

She told him, although not in particularly great detail. It wasn't, after all, anything terribly exciting.

'And what did you think of the place?' he asked when she'd finished, asking not as if he really cared, but simply because the question was more or less expected.

Holly couldn't resist it. 'Well, it's a nice enough place to visit, but I'm not sure I'd like to live here,' she replied, following the lines of a gag so old she wasn't sure where it might have originated.

Wade might have known, but he didn't join her laughter. Instead, somewhat to her surprise, his eyes narrowed fractionally and one eyebrow lifted in a look that might have been speculative. But it was all done so quickly she didn't know what interpretation to put on it.

'Hmmmm. Well, maybe you haven't seen the right parts yet,' he said finally. 'We'll see about fixing that up today. If nothing else maybe it'll give us both something else to think about.'

'I'll need to know more than that,' Holly said. 'Or were you serious about putting on a swimsuit?' Of course he wasn't, she thought, only to be proved wrong.

'Certainly,' he said with a slow grin. 'Can you think of anything you look better in?'

'I certainly can, and what's more, I'm not going anywhere for lunch in a swimsuit.' Damn the man anyway; why did he have this uncanny ability to fluster her? How could he make her temper so fragile with so little obvious effort?

Worse, he seemed impervious to her moods. 'Well, I had presumed you'd take along something to throw on over it after our swim,' he grinned. 'Not that it'll matter a great deal; we're going for the tucker, not the social standing.'

'Well that's better, sort of,' she conceded. 'So we're going somewhere to swim, and then for lunch. Anywhere else?'

Wade grinned again, this time with definite mischief in his eyes. 'Ah, now I see,' he said. 'Expecting me to lead you down the garden path, take you somewhere you might feel uncomfortable because of the way you're dressed.' His eyes roamed boldly across her figure, lingering on the deep neckline of her robe, then wandering down to the curve of her ankles. 'Why Holly, would I do that?' And the question answered itself. He could and he would, if it suited him. But not now, not having warned her. Holly didn't dignify it with a reply.

'Right,' he said, still grinning mischievously. 'So let's get on with it; we've got a fair ways to go. You've got ten minutes and then I'll be in to help you figure what to wear.'

And he rose from his chair like some great cat, striding to the door without a backward glance. Holly scampered to her room, threw on a bikini and a light beach jacket, then had to scramble to find her handbag and a pair of low-heeled sandals she'd bought the day before. She thought seriously of taking jeans and a tank-top in her beach-bag, but before she could collect them she heard Wade knocking at the door, his every knock a threat of intrusion into her fragile privacy.

Wade drove silently through the town to the main north-south coastal highway, a few minutes later, and eventually said, 'I expect you to take due and proper consideration for the change in scenery as we get along a bit. Hedland's situated rather in the middle of nothing, but once you get a ways away from it, the country starts to show its true colours.'

And it did! Much to Holly's surprise, they travelled only a short distance south of Port Hedland before suddenly finding a landscape in a state of change. At first she could hardly believe her eyes as the subtlety of soft-coloured ranges began to float into view over the heat haze. They seemed unreal, disembodied. But as the speeding, air-conditioned car sped closer, the ranges of hills took on more substance, although their colouring remained so soft, so muted by distance, heat haze and the harsh sunlight that she found herself wondering if they hadn't somehow been transformed from another planet.

Everything was red or purple or some shade between. Even in the distant mauve of the hills was a tinge of red, just enough to draw the eye. It was beautiful, and yet . . .

'It's so . . . so empty,' she ventured, meaning it not as a criticism. But she drew only a grunt from the driver. Wade obviously didn't consider her vocal opinions terribly important. Or was it her choice of words? Clearly he had his own love for this vast, widespread land where distance only added to the beauty.

As they sped southward, Holly was consciously reminded of the descriptions in the Zane Grey westerns she'd read as a child. Purple, and in all shades and tones, now seemed to dominate the landscape. It subjugated the pale, dusty green of the spinifex bushes that covered the ground so sparsely, shading away to red wherever the soil colour could force a way through to the sunlight.

Wade continued to drive in silence, only speaking when he bothered to point out the gentle, eighty-six-metre slope of Mount Berghaus and the slightly higher rise of two-hundred-and-four-metre Mount Constantine.

What impressed Holly the most, as they continued south, was the incredible, changeable beauty the barren landscape seemed to create with every kilometre they travelled. And yet it was a harsh, unforgiving land, a rugged, seemingly tireless place in which Holly could feel herself an intruder even as was the bitumen highway and the modern vehicle in which they travelled. That impression was reinforced when Wade turned off on to a broad, gravel track at a signpost marked 'Cossack'.

Cossack, he informed her, was now a ghost town, only the skeleton of its former glory as one of the region's earliest settlements. 'You'll have to use your imagination to appreciate it,' he said, and when they arrived, Holly could understand what he meant.

The tiny, abandoned settlement with its clutches of stone and brick buildings—many of them in surprisingly good shape for their age—had an almost ethereal quality in the brilliance of the tropical sunlight.

The old courthouse, looking almost as if ready for business, the hotel with its ancient empty ovens now only a showplace for graffiti, and the roofless cell blocks with massive iron doors still firmly in place ... it was incredibly lovely despite the loneliness that hung over the place like a shroud.

'This was to have been the centre of the Northwest,' Wade mused. 'Only the estuary silted up, and without a decent harbour, that was the beginning of the end.'

She could understand his meaning, but in her own heart was only astonishment at the hardiness of those pioneers who'd created a town from the raw rock around them, only to find it useless, and finally to leave it, leaving their hopes, their dreams, their children's futures.

When Wade advised her that there was a move afoot, finally, to ensure the preservation of Cossack as an historic town, she felt a surge of gladness. Nothing with so much history, so much tragedy, should be allowed to disappear without at least a second chance, Holly thought.

'It'll take a lot of time and a lot of money,' Wade said as if reading her thoughts, 'but I reckon it has to be worth it. Lord, they must have been a tough breed, those original pioneers. People think the Northwest is tough now, but then ...'

Holly was barely listening; her attention was drawn instead to the enormous statue that seemed to dominate the former village centre of Cossack. She had noticed the statue on their arrival, of course, but now, having seen the stark evidence of civilisation's first feeble hold upon the region, the statue seemed to take on new emphasis.

It was a life-sized portrayal of four figures, roughly hewn but the more beautiful for that. A pioneer, standing and gazing out to sea over the now-silted estuary, while his wife and child sat beside him and an Aboriginal tracker sat at his feet. Already weathered by the harshness of the climate, the statue seemed none the less indomitable, like the land itself.

Or like Wade! Or was that only her imagination that saw so much of his rugged individuality in the stern face of the statue? Certainly, Holly thought, there was little of the brittle Ramona Mason revealed in the female portion of the statue. This woman was a true mother-figure, tough, solid, enduring.

Then she chuckled at her cattiness. Whatever would make her think such things? Wade, thankfully, didn't appear to notice. But that didn't make the realisation any easier to handle. Holly was glad when he finally decided they should return to the car and continue their expedition.

She was equally glad to accept his expression of concern for her own comfort. The sun, he maintained, was growing hotter to the point where he thought she'd appreciate the return to the vehicle's air-conditioning.

'Well, I'll have to get used to it sometime,' she replied without thinking. Then could have shrieked at his reply.

'Easier said than done. It takes years,' he said, and might as well have damned her on the spot. What Holly heard was a different message—'You won't be here long enough for it to matter.' She made that interpretation also by herself, and replied somewhat acidly.

'It hasn't really been decided, has it?' she countered briskly, attempting to brazen her way through the iciness inside her. 'At the very least, we'll have to wait and see how Jessica fares, unless of course you're so anxious to get rid of me that . . .'

'What *are* you on about?' he interrupted. 'Nobody, least of all me, is trying to get rid of you. Now stop trying to create an issue where one doesn't exist.' His tones revealed boredom, but Holly knew better. He wasn't bored, merely resigned to her presence. But then, why all this trouble to show her around? It did seem he was carrying hospitality a bit further than was required. Unless, of course, he too was so worried about Jessica that he'd make any excuse to get away from the house, from the tension of the telephone.

'I hope it's only the fact that you're thirsty that makes you so stroppy,' he said then with a surprisingly warm grin. 'We'll stop at the lookout for a tinnie; maybe the walk will give you an appetite as well, because you're going to need it, I can assure you of that.'

The lookout turned out to be a tiny, roofed pergola that perched on top of a steep bluff, giving a shaded over-view of the coast from the Cossack inlet to the rugged coastline of the Dampier Archipelago a few miles to the south of them.

It was a curious place, high and windswept and vulnerable, yet commanding sweeping views of astounding loveliness. Below them, the sea was a perfect tropical turquoise, with the height making it possible to pick out each slightly darker or lighter area of reef or sandbank.

But it was, as Wade had promised, a bit of a walk from the car and very steep, so when he snapped open a can of beer and offered it to her, Holly found the golden liquid more refreshing than she'd expected. The can was empty almost as soon as she'd begun it, but Wade seemed to find that perfectly normal, and merely handed her another one without even being asked.

'But that's all you get for now,' he said with a teasing grin. 'I don't want you falling down tipsy during lunch.'

'Well, I should certainly hope not,' Holly agreed, but was none the less grateful for his supporting hand as they descended the narrow track to the car park.

What followed was only a short drive by comparison to the distance they'd already come. They cut the corner of the small community of Wickham, then continued on to Point Samson. Wade kept up a touristy commentary as they drove, pointing out the various sights in a cheerful, running patter that seemed to Holly to reveal a definite change of mood. Where he'd seemed merely polite earlier in the day, he now seemed positively cheerful, although Holly silently reminded herself not to be fooled. Wade Bannister, she knew only too well, was not a man to be taken for granted about anything, not even his temperament.

After skirting the edge of Point Samson, they arrived at a parking area significant only for the enormous, rusting, abandoned boilers that seemed to litter the landscape. The place looked to Holly like some giant's junkyard.

'Doesn't look like much, does it?' Wade chuckled. 'But don't be fooled. It's a dandy place for swimming, among other things.'

The look in his eye was clear enough, but Holly was already halfway through asking 'What other things?' before she realised she was being baited yet again. His grin before responding was positively devilish.

'It's called Honeymoon Cove,' he said. 'Figure it out for yourself.'

'I shan't bother,' she retorted with a toss of her head. 'The swimming will be quite sufficient for me, thank you.'

'Oh, I'm sure it would be,' was his reply, but when Holly turned to seek confirmation of the answer's suggestiveness, there was nothing in his eyes or face to confirm her impression.

'You just remember to watch where you put your feet, although it's usually quite safe here,' he reminded her. 'And if you see a sea snake or a Noah's ark—or hear me calling a warning—don't hang about asking questions, just get out of it fast.'

Noah's ark ... shark, her memory translated, but her voice showed concern when she asked, 'Sea snakes?' Wade was already slipping out of his clothing, revealing a body so hard and bronzed it made Holly feel like a washed-out sickling by comparison.

'Yes, there might be a few around, but there are seldom many here, and the sharks usually stay well out. It's a nice, protected little cove,' he replied, stepping over to help Holly out of the beach jacket that covered her bikini.

As Holly turned to face him, she found something in his eyes that belied her own impressions about how she must look.

'Don't worry, little Hollyhock. I won't let anything hurt you,' Wade said in a voice strangely gentle, even more strangely alluring, persuasive. Then he took her hand and led her down the narrow walkway to the cove. Holly followed like a child, fearless and trusting.

The beach at Honeymoon Cove was only a small nook, carved by the sea from towering expanses of jagged dark rock that ran around the convoluted coastline from the long Point Samson jetty. The footpath traversed the weathered surfaces of the rock, but to step off it in bare feet would have meant precarious going.

And yet it was beautiful, that dark, sea-burnished surface. In places, the waves had carved tunnels and gorges towards the shore, revealing twisting, sculptured walls in a variety of colours and gradually collecting a carpet of bright pebbles in the bottoms of the fluted chambers.

Dumping towels and beach gear on a handy rock ledge. Wade plunged confidently into the slow, gentle waves. Holly followed more cautiously, one eye anxiously scanning the placid, turquoise water for sea snakes and the other following Wade's bronzed, athletic figure.

The water deepened so gradually that they were far out before it was even waist deep, and Holly thought they could almost walk to the tiny islet that perched some distance off shore. But clearly Wade had no such intention; he was content to swim lazily back and forth, relaxing in the warm, basking sea and—Holly was certain—watching her as she tried to shrug off her nervousness and swim with some equal pleasure. If only he hadn't mentioned sharks and sea snakes, it would have been easier, she thought.

Floating, finally, on her back, eyes roving the blue heavens above as she watched the passing sea birds and puff balls of soft cloud, she found herself wondering if it really was possible that Wade was changing his mind about her. She wanted him to, no sense in trying to deny that. But he was so damned insular, so difficult to predict and even more so to interpret.

His feelings for Jessica were open enough, as were his feelings for the Northwest, his home. But with Holly herself, he seemed to carry unpredictability as a shield she couldn't breach.

It just wasn't fair, she thought. She'd explained the incident at the airport, and he really had nothing else against her. Except, perhaps, the situation of the rented equipment for his party. But then Jessica had clarified that, surely? Was it that he just didn't trust her, had some strange, instinctive barrier against her? That was a possibility Holly didn't really care to consider.

Turning her head, she glanced across to where he was sliding porpoise-like through the gentle waves, his body gleaming as the flashes of salt water shimmered along the muscular torso, the long, well-shaped legs. How at home he seemed in the sea, Holly thought, remembering how equally at home he'd seemed once they'd left the built-up area of Port Hedland and driven into the heat-hazed emptiness beyond.

Would his children be equally at home here in this vast, desolate, beautiful isolation? She supposed so, and wondered almost in the same breath if they might also be *her* children. Realisation of that radical thought was so shocking that Holly gasped in surprise, almost tipping herself off balance.

She looked across at him again, glad he hadn't been able to notice her momentary surprise, much less guess the reason for it!

At first she saw only his imperious upraised hand. A gesture unmistakable in its message—Stay Still! Then she saw, flashing through the water between them in deadly undulations, the sinister, writhing shape that could only be a sea snake.

Holly's mouth opened to scream, but she was unbalanced and got only a mouthful of water that doubled her panic. She thrashed, blind and deaf with panic, her choking intensified and the salt water in her eyes obscuring her vision. She tried again to scream, but only a helpless gurgle emerged; she tried to stand upright, but where was *up?*

And then she was being grabbed, her body forcibly held against the writhing of her panic, which grew as the physical constraints increased.

'Damn it, woman . . . be still! You're all right. All right!'

She heard the words, but her brain refused to comprehend. She struggled even harder, lashing out with hands and feet in a frenzy as she fought her freedom.

'Holly! Stop it!' This time the voice was sharper still, knifing through her struggles. Iron bands closed around her arms, binding them to her sides, cutting off her breath until exhaustion halted her writhing, frantic struggle.

'Good girl. It's all right . . . it's all right.' The voice droned on, softer now, enticing, protecting. The bands loosened until she could breathe more freely, yet held her secure and upright. She could feel the warm water against her lips, her legs, but her face was clear now, the air coming into her lungs was fresh and dry.

She coughed, tried vainly to writhe free once more, but found herself caught up like a child in arms that cradled her with the same gentleness as was in the voice.

'Easy, easy love. Nobody's going to hurt you. Relax.'

She opened her eyes to find his own startling green eyes only inches away, staring down at her with unbelievable tenderness that caught in her throat worse than the gulped-in sea water. Wade was holding her close against his broad chest, and she then became conscious of his easy, flowing walk as he plodded towards the distant sand of the beach.

Holly closed her eyes for an instant, and when she looked again his expression had changed totally. Still warm, but gone was that exquisite tenderness, that heart-melting softness. Has she merely imagined it?

'Bloody stupid woman,' he growled in mock anger, shaking his head and smiling to show he wasn't really serious. 'Why the hell couldn't you have just stayed still like I told you? The thing was headed away from you, after all.'

She shuddered at the thought of the writhing marine snake, unable to contain a renewed surge of terror. How could she possibly explain to this man, born and raised to accept such dangers as normal, how utterly frightening, how totally unnerving that single sea snake had been to her? No matter which way it was going!

The futility brought immediate anger, and she twisted in his grasp, her lips curling as she snapped, 'I wouldn't expect you to understand. Put me down!'

'Put you down?' There was mockery in his eyes now, his arms closing even tighter around her slender figure.

'Yes! Put me down—right this very minute!' Holly spat out the command, knowing even as she did that she might as well have saved her breath. Issuing a command to Wade Bannister, she realised, was exactly the wrong approach—unless she wanted him to do just the opposite.

'I think I'd rather hang on to you,' he drawled, mischief twisting the corners of his generous mouth. 'It isn't every day I get to hold such a tasty morsel, and on such an aptly named beach, too.'

He grinned down at her shamelessly, and Holly noticed that he'd stopped his approach to the beach. Indeed, he was turned around and seemed headed back out to sea. Out to sea—where there were undoubtedly a thousand more sea snakes! She tried to object, but her voice emerged as a tiny shriek.

'Wh . . . what are you doing?' she finally managed to stammer, her eyes fearfully scanning the turquoise waters as her arms clasped convulsively about his corded neck.

He merely chuckled, deliberately taunting. 'I'm taking you back where I got you from, of course,' he said, and Holly could tell that he meant it, that he was now enjoying every single instant of the torture.

Even as she realised that, he relaxed the arm beneath

her knees, allowing her to slide into an upright position against him. And he was deep, so deep that her feet couldn't touch bottom.

Instinctively, her arms locked around his neck. The last thing she now wanted was to be released, although she could hardly say so. Not in the face of that mocking grin. No, that would just be playing right into his hands, not that it could matter much; she was there already.

She felt his hands close around her waist, the long fingers shifting to bring her close against him, holding her body against the warmth of his, hip to hip, thigh against thigh. Then his fingers moved, enticingly caressing the small of her back, tracing the nubbles of her lower spine, the soft swell of her buttocks.

A moan escaped her, a moan created by the sheer bliss of his touch, by the involuntary, inescapable reaction of her body to his. She felt the moist heat of him through the touching of their skins, the brush of his chest hair teasing her nipples into firmness through the bikini top. And lower, the hardness that told her she wasn't the only one so aroused by the way they were linked in the water.

His fingers were creators of esctasy, each of them brushing at the fineness of her skin like a artist's brush, and her own fingers tangled in the wet hair at his nape, tugging to pull his head down, to force his lips to meet her own.

'Wade . . .' It was a sigh, a plea, a cry of desperation so soft she wasn't totally aware of having uttered it. His fingers pressed at her hips and her legs parted to let him closer to the core of her being.

Her lips were at his throat now, nibbling, exploring the strength she found there, the tautness of muscle, the slight rasp of beard as she moved her lips upward, seeking his mouth.

Around them, the water was like a warm bath, enveloping them, helping to heat the passion that flowed like a current when their mouths met. Holly felt herself being turned round, felt his fingers as they left her back to trace delicate lines across the tops of her breasts before gently freeing them from the restraint of the bikini top.

And then she was being lifted as if by a wave to give his lips access, lips that teased and thrilled, a tongue that touched like a hot iron at the tips of her nipples, then curled in expert agony to bring them to even more rigid attention.

And even as he lifted her, his hands continued in their riotous, delightful exploration, mirrored by the fluttering path of her own fingers down the drift of his chest, across the muscled flatness of his stomach.

She wanted him. All of him, And now, here, enveloped in the ageless rhythm of the sea, a rhythm that seemed somehow just right for their first complete, total lovemaking. And he wanted her; no longer any doubt about that. It seemed no longer significant what past mistakes, what past misunderstandings might have separated them. All that could matter now to Holly was . . . now!

'Oh, God . . . Wade . . . love me,' she cried as his fingers played at the edges of her bikini, fingers that somehow put a delaying on the surge of passion that shook through her. 'Now!' she cried louder, but his reply, if there had been one, was lost in the flow of her hair across his mouth.

Lost—then truly lost in the far-off sound of a car door slamming, followed by the excited shrieks of children racing down the footpath to the beach.

'Damn,' Holly cried, and this time felt his echo even as his fingers changed from pleasure to practised efficiency as he helped her to readjust her swimsuit.

But when she finally met his eyes, it was as if some shutter had been drawn across them, hiding from her whatever he'd been feeling that moment before, that infinite lifetime ago. His eyes now were like mirrors, revealing all of her own emotions, but hiding all of his.

CHAPTER EIGHT

THEY lunched at Moby's Kitchen, staring out across the brilliant green gardens to the sea beyond, each of them lost in thoughts apparently destined to remain unshared. They lunched on exquisitely prepared prawns and squid and delicately flavoured reef fish and it might have been hamburger for all Holly cared.

What had they almost done, out there in the warm, soft water of Honeymoon Cove? What had they somehow, through a slip of circumstance, missed? And would she ever, she now wondered, have the chance to regain that intimacy, that sense of having truly been loved, cherished, wanted?

If he'd said he was sorry, she'd have cried, although she'd desperately wanted him to say something, anything, to help restore her thoroughly shattered composure. Instead, he had taken her hand and steadied her as they moved to where Holly's own rubbery legs could carry her beside him to the beach, where he'd actually smiled and waved at the intruding children, then walked beside her to the car, helped her to dry off and get into her beach coat.

Damn the man! Nobody should have such control. It wasn't fair; it wasn't even human.

Even looking across the table at Wade, she could feel her tummy flutter with the coals of her passion, carefully banked but never to be allowed to die. And she knew beyond caring that she loved him, she wanted him, and—perhaps—would never have him. Not even just as a lover. Not now. Somehow, he'd changed since that forever-ago moment in the water, and now he seemed more removed from her than ever.

She drank the wine he'd bought, ate the lightly battered delicacies of the sea—*his* sea—and cursed herself for a fool, for having been such a fool as to let herself be drawn into that horrid, never-to-be-forgotten airport conversation, and could have wept for the way she knew she'd feel tomorrow, and perhaps all the tomorrows after that. It was all so futile, so exhaustingly, bitterly frustrating.

And Wade's actions and attitude didn't make things any easier. He was polite, courteous, even entertaining during the drive home that afternoon. They stopped at the Whim Creek pub for a cooling drink, and there he was even amusing, relating a variety of anecdotes about the isolated pub.

He bought her a stubby cooler, a plastic cup filled with insulating material, designed to keep beer bottles from warming too quickly in the hot, dry climate. On the outside of it was a cartoon drawing in which one typical Pilbara local complained to another about how the country was filling up with people and development. Taken in the context of Whim Creek's isolation—it was the only building, practically, for miles in any direction—the point would have been amusing if Holly had been in the mood to be amused.

But to her it represented only a tangible reminder of her visit, notwithstanding the fact that her own memory and that of her body would be tangible enough. Could she ever forget Honeymoon Cove? Certainly, she realised, it would be easier to forget than Wade Bannister, whose touch seemed branded into her skin, whose voice was imprinted into her consciousness.

They had barely got into the house that evening when the telephone started ringing, obviating any thought Holly might have entertained about trying to talk to Wade, trying to see if he mightn't vocalise his vivid mood swing, her own feelings.

The first call was obviously work. Holly couldn't even understand half the technical jargon involved, and paid little attention overall. The second call seemed similar, in that Wade promised to be there first thing in the morning and refused to estimate how long he'd require to be there.

However important that problem might have been, it just disappeared from her mind a moment later, when the telephone rang again and Wade, after answering, immediately motioned Holly closer.

'It's Perth—finally,' he muttered, then stared at her in silence, the strain revealed in every line of his face, until finally the party trying to contact him came on the line.

Wade spoke seldom during the exchange that followed, and Holly's impatience grew increasingly obvious as she struggled to comprehend the one-sided conversation. It seemed an hour before he finally offered his thanks and hung up the phone.

'Well thank God for that,' he began, only to have her interrupt with a strident demand for detailed, specific information.

'Patience,' he said calmingly, 'is a virtue.' And his expression seemed to indicate that Holly could be more virtuous in other areas, as well. Or was that her conscience speaking? Either way, it served only to heighten her anger.

'Yes! Well we know that I don't have much of that, don't we?' she countered, and immediately repeated her original demand. 'What's happening with Jessica, damn it?'

'My, my . . . aren't we touchy?' he replied scathingly. 'Now really, Holly, I think you should drop this martyred act. It's distinctly bad for your disposition, not to mention the peace and harmony of this household.'

'Martyr? You wouldn't know a martyr if it jumped

up and bit you in the . . .' Holly squealed. 'Oh, never mind. I'm past caring what you think of me. All I want to know is the truth about Jessica's condition. Or is that too much to ask?'

'Of course not, although where I come from, ladies say *please*,' he replied, voice maddeningly calm and an unholy gleam of almost malicious pleasure in his eyes at the torment he was causing her. It was obvious Jessica wasn't in any great danger, but damn him, that was no excuse for teasing.

'All right. Please. Please, please, please.' Holly's voice was resigned, heavy with exasperation. But to her great surprise he accepted the surrender and immediately launched into a detailed account.

'So it isn't nearly as bad as it might have been, though she's to have no visitors until Monday,' he said. 'Which means I'll have to try and get back Sunday night so we can go together—although if I don't make it, you must go by yourself, of course.'

'What? And leave the house unattended?' The words were out, venomous in their sarcasm, almost before Holly realised it, and the flash of anger in his eyes showed how close to the nerve she'd struck.

Then he merely sighed deeply, the sigh of a patient parent, Holly thought. '*I'll* worry about that,' he said. 'And I promise you'll be on that plane even if it means I have to stay back myself to keep an eye on the bloody house. Okay?'

'Now who's being a martyr?' Holly retorted, smiling widely to show she was trying to make amends for her own earlier testiness. 'Look, I'm sorry to be so edgy. It's just that . . .'

'It's just that you're as worried about Jessica as I am, and yes, of course I realise it,' he interrupted. Then paused before continuing.

'But she is in the very best possible hands; the

operation was as successful as could be expected, and we're both tired and we're both cranky. So let's just leave it there. If I'm not back in time, you hop on that plane without a second thought. And no arguments, either, not that I expect any.'

'Yes, sir. Whatever you say, sir,' Holly agreed with a warm smile that she hoped might ease his tense anger.

'And don't be cheeky. Just do as you're told,' he snapped, although she sensed his anger wasn't entirely with her. He then spent nearly an hour sorting out their flight arrangements and writing a list of directions for Holly so she could find her way if he didn't get back in time to accompany her.

Then, while Holly put together a light supper, Wade went off to organise himself for his business journey the next day. It was an activity that seemed to do nothing whatsoever for his temperament, she thought when the meal was over and neither of them had eaten enough to justify the effort involved.

Several times that evening she felt he was on the verge of saying something, but each time he seemingly backed away from that precipice, leaving Holly increasingly angry and frustrated. He's probably trying to work up the right words to tell me just to stay in Perth, or even pack up Jessica and take her back to England with me, Holly thought sadly.

Under the circumstances, she could hardly burst forth with a revelation of her own, especially not the admission that she was in love with Wade, in love with the Pilbara, and would never, by choice, leave either of them. Such an admission, however, might not only be foolhardy and fruitless, but self-demeaning to a degree she just couldn't accept. It was one thing, she decided, to swallow one's pride, but quite another to have it rammed down one's throat.

Her sleep that night was troubled, a kaleidoscope of

nightmares that trampled on the replays of her erotic
incident at Honeymoon Cove, then trampled even more
firmly on whatever dreams of the future she might dare
to entertain. She was up well before dawn, and had
coffee going and breakfast ready to cook when Wade
arrived with the first rays of sunlight.

'You couldn't sleep either, I take it,' he commented,
not waiting for a reply before adding, 'I had a helluva
night.' But it was what followed that surprised Holly
beyond belief.

'I expect it was guilt that kept me awake,' he said.
'I'm sorry, Holly, for taking advantage of you
yesterday.'

She could hardly believe her ears. How on earth
could he imagine he'd been taking advantage? It wasn't,
after all, as if she'd been attempting to repulse his
advances. Anything but!

She found herself tempted to reply that she was only
sorry he hadn't taken *more* advantage, but she bit off
that comment just in time by making one equally
dangerous. 'I certainly wouldn't have expected you to
lose any sleep over it,' she quipped, and immediately
could have kicked herself.

'Well, I did. And although I'm pleased you don't
seem to be holding a grudge, I should have realised how
unfair it was to play silly games when you were just as
worried as I was. It was boorish and quite rude of me
not to have just told you straightaway about Jessica's
situation, and I apologise for not doing so.'

Holly didn't know whether to laugh or cry. 'Oh!' It
was the only thing she could say, and immediately she
wished she'd held back that expression of surprise. How
stupid!

Here she'd assumed he was apologising for having
almost seduced her, and all he was concerned with was
having mildly tormented her. Probably, she thought,

he'd laugh himself sick at the idea of her thinking he'd apologise for his lovemaking. He'd probably, in all honesty, be more likely to apologise for having stopped when he did.

'Like I said, I wouldn't lose any sleep over it,' she finally managed to reply, trying desperately to hold back her tears and keep her voice as expressionless as possible. Then she turned away and began preparing their breakfast, unwilling to acknowledge the narrow, speculative glance he shot at her in response.

They ate in a prickly silence that wasn't improved by Holly's own feelings of false domesticity at the scene. How wonderful it would be, she thought, to always be in the position of sharing breakfast with this man. Then she thrust the idea from her mind. It was ludicrous to torture herself; Wade Bannister couldn't and wouldn't ever have the type of feelings for Holly that she had for him, especially not with Ramona Mason at his beck and call.

Only, why did he insist on pinning her with that curious, speculative glance whenever she chanced to look up? Damn him, why couldn't he just finish up and go?

But no. First he had to have another cup of coffee, and then another cigarette. And all the time, those compelling green eyes followed her like a shadow. If he didn't leave soon, she'd do something, or say something quite drastic, Holly thought.

'Are you going to miss me?'

The question arrived without warning, without even the slightest indicated preliminaries. Holly was so surprised it took her a moment to comprehend what he'd asked, and, having comprehended, to supply a safe answer.

'Only if we have a cyclone,' she finally shrugged, then hurried on, her mouth running away with her in a desperate bid to protect her fragile ego. 'I'm still not totally confident about my ability to cope, but then I don't suppose there's much risk of a cyclone in the next few days anyway. Is there?'

Wade didn't answer at once. He sat regarding her with a curious expression in his eyes, and when he did speak, there was something in his voice that might almost have been defensive.

'That wasn't exactly what I meant,' he said slowly, then rose without warning in a gesture that seemed to dismiss the subject entirely. 'This isn't the time, any more than—well, I think we can leave the rest of this discussion until I get back,' he said then. 'You take care, little Hollyhock.'

His lips brushed across hers in a gesture that could have meant anything, and he was out the door before she could even think to reply. By the time Holly recovered sufficiently to follow, he was already backing his truck from the garage.

'Now don't forget. If I'm not back before that plane goes on Monday morning, I want *you* on it,' he ordered, and drove off before she could reply. It was almost, Holly decided, as if he was insisting on always having the last word. Decidedly frustrating, almost as frustrating as having to remain here in Port Hedland while Jessica, who needed her, was in Perth and Wade, who apparently didn't need her at all, was somewhere else. Where?

'The least he might have done was tell me where he was going,' she muttered over a third cup of coffee she didn't really want and subsequently almost spilled when the jangling telephone startled her from her black thoughts.

'Oh, it's ... uhm ... Holly, is it?' asked a brittle, vaguely familiar voice when she answered the phone. 'I suppose Wade's already left then?'

Ramona Mason hardly waited for a reply, and seemed almost put out at Holly's immediate attempt at an explanation. 'No, there's no need to leave a message,' she said somewhat petulantly. 'I'll be seeing him soon enough that it would hardly make any sense. But tell me, dear, what have you heard about your aunt? Is everything all right now?'

The tones were so condescending, so smarmily patronising, that Holly had to bite her tongue. So this damned blonde was being kept informed about Jessica's circumstances, while she had to drag every report out of Wade as if she were pulling teeth. The nerve! But she forced herself to be polite, and gave Ramona the barest details in a voice she hardly recognised as her own. The reply was unexpected, to say the least.

'Monday? Oh, how perfect,' Ramona said. 'I'll have to be sure and take her in some flowers. And I'm sure Wade . . . and you, too, of course, must be pleased. I do hope the news causes some improvement in his temperament; the last few times I've seen him, he's been, oh—but of course you'd know that, wouldn't you? At any rate, I'll find out for myself when I see him today.'

Ramona rang off with a hasty farewell, and it wasn't until she'd put the telephone down that Holly realised the call had been preceded by the bleeps that indicated a long-distance call, dialled direct.

Holly's heart sank; the bottom dropped out of her world with the realisation of what Ramona's call must mean. Wade wouldn't be coming back on Sunday because he was already on his way to Perth. To see Ramona, no doubt, but also to be there to see Jessica—without Holly!

Then she began to rationalise, although the curtain of white-hot, growing anger made it difficult. How could he? Too easily; he need only drive to the airport, leave his vehicle there or somewhere handy, and be gone. Or else drive to Karratha and pick up a plane there.

Leaving me to babysit his stupid house while he plays the concerned employer, Holly thought savagely. And with Ramona Mason to fill in the time between visits. She had been well-and-truly led down the garden path, Holly thought, as the implications became more and more obvious in her mind.

Suddenly furious, she snatched up the telephone again and dialled the airport, demanding a seat on the first flight to Perth. It was seven calls later, having exhausted every single alternative, that she was forced to accept that the only seat available was the one already booked for her on Monday morning.

She could go stand-by, but every authority assured her that the list was so long she'd be wiser to await her scheduled flight.

A bus? The thought resulted in several more telephone calls and the information—already known—that shift changes on one of the large Northwest Shelf oil drilling crews had cornered every possible form of transportation, bar hitch-hiking.

She was angry enough to try it, but not silly enough. No, she'd wait for Monday morning, but when she saw Wade Bannister again she'd have a few new words to teach him, and they weren't nice words at all.

She thought about those words throughout the day and evening, while her mood swings ranged from blackest depression to near hysteria. How could he do such a thing? And how could she still love a man she now hated and despised? It was senseless.

By noon the next day she was so confused, so bitterly angry and bored and frustrated that hitch-hiking began to look viable after all. She'd cleaned the house, weeded the garden, done all the laundry and read half the books in the house. Or at least, pretended to read them while half her mind was busy composing confrontation scenes with Wade.

She hadn't bothered with the radio or television, and as she was chewing her way through a tasteless lunch, realised she'd been totally out of touch with world affairs since the weekend. She reached across to flip on the radio, then almost recoiled as the first word she heard was *his* name!

'. . . Wade is now six hundred kilometres northwest of Port Hedland and moving in a southeasterly direction at approximately sixty kilometres an hour,' the announcer's voice said. 'A cyclone watch will continue for coastal communities between Broome and Exmouth . . .'

Holly didn't wait to hear the rest. She rushed quickly to peer with astonishment at the clear, sunny skies outside, while *his* name reverberated inside her skull.

It was some sort of ghastly joke! Surely, it must be, the weather outside was identical to what had occurred every day since her arrival. The sky was cloudless and blue, the sun a growing fireball, and there was no more than the usual light breeze to stir the foliage in the garden.

And . . . Cyclone *Wade*? How ironically fitting, she thought, then shivered despite the warmth. Ironic, but hardly fitting. Suddenly Holly felt terribly, vulnerably alone. How could she cope if the cyclone did come to Port Hedland? She had no real experience, only what she'd read and heard. It couldn't possibly be enough.

But likely it wouldn't matter. Cyclones were reputedly erratic, and this one still had a long way to go before it would threaten Port Hedland or anywhere else in Australia. According to everything she'd learned, it could turn away in any direction and at any moment, and the odds against a direct hit were comforting.

Holly told herself that over and over again as she

worked her way through the routine of preparing for that remote possibility. It would have been much easier not to worry, she thought, if it weren't for the name they'd chosen, and it was little consolation to remember Wade himself saying that cyclone names were drawn out of a hat each year and assigned to the various states without preference. Coincidence, Holly decided, was unnerving regardless of how it occurred.

The worst part of it all was simply the waiting. In her imagination, she had always thought of cyclones as whirlwinds of disaster, dervishes that struck like lightning, struck without warning. There was some consolation in having found that yes, such cyclones did exist—Tracy had smashed Darwin virtually without warning in 1974—but the majority gave warning after warning after warning as they developed slowly from their births as tropical low-pressure systems.

Apart from the routine precautions, all of which had been done long before Holly's arrival, most of what was left to do could be left until the cyclone—*her* cyclone, she thought—had matured to the point where cyclone warnings were begun.

What would Wade think, she pondered, if he returned early to find that she'd already prepared herself for a cyclone that hadn't even justified warnings? Probably he'd understand, and equally probably he'd laugh.

And he'd think she was just a typical flighty female, shying at shadows and over-reacting. Certainly not the type to be living here in this beautiful, rugged region where cyclones were something to be expected, endured and recovered from.

Then she remembered that he wouldn't be returning early; he'd be comfortably curled up with Ramona Mason somewhere in Perth, probably laughing at Holly's predicament as he watched the television weather forecasts.

Well, too bad, she thought, carefully packing up the remainder of his book collection in plastic bags and checking for the hundredth time that every cyclone shutter was secure. If Wade chose to think of her as a panic merchant, even to laugh at her, it would have to be borne. Jessica would be doing this, and Holly knew she must uphold the family standard despite her own thoughts of abandoning everything of Wade's to the elements. It would serve him right, too, but of course she couldn't do it.

Nor did she have any chance to vent her emotions against him in person, because of course he hadn't returned when the first proper cyclone warning emerged from the radio in funereal tones that struck like a death knell at Holly's imagination.

By this time she was more than ready. The tiny bathroom-cum-cyclone shelter was loaded down with emergency gear: candles, first-aid supplies, food, large plastic water containers, everything suggested in the town's natural disaster counter-plan.

And yet, the sky outside remained blue and the descending sun was as tropically brilliant as ever. Except that now on the horizon there was a tiny slurry of grey smudging the edges of the sky. Or was it her imagination?

No. Although the winds were still light, they were stronger than the usual evening breeze, and even as she watched, the grey smudge drew nearer, thicker, blacker. Yet there was no hint of rain, or of the cyclonic winds that could gust to two hundred kilometres an hour, destroying everything they touched.

And the warnings continued. Now the tracking facilities indicated the cyclone might strike within twenty-four hours, anywhere between Broome and Dampier with the most likely landfall somewhere to the north in the sparsely inhabited region between Port Hedland and Broome.

Unless it turned. Unless it changed direction. Unless . . .

Holly ate dinner late, for once taking a thoroughly interested view as the television weather people detailed the movements of her cyclone. She cleared up the dishes slowly, filling in the immensity of waiting time until the last glass was spotless, the final piece of cutlery gleaming.

Then she took herself out to sit under the roof of the patio, where she sprawled in a lounge chair and watched as the stars slowly disappeared beneath a blanket of cloud that was visible only at the leading edge. Her smudge had grown, was continuing to grow. And Wade was . . . where?

Cyclone Wade, she knew, was somewhere to the northwest and spinning in a great, clockwise spiral, perhaps a thousand metres high, perhaps twelve thousand. But her Wade—or more properly Ramona's Wade, she thought bitterly—where was he? Could he really intend to let her go through the terror of this cyclone alone? In her heart, she couldn't believe that, but what else was there to think?

The first drop of rain splattered down at exactly 1:14 a.m. the next day. Holly saw it, noted the time, and watched as it was joined by another drop, then another and another, watched as the drops seemed to merge, uniting to make larger drops, growing to build a wash of water that quickly grew heavier and heavier. There were no more stars now, only the sodden blackness above that eventually diminished to a more sodden greyness as the dawn struggled to throw light through the curtain of the rain many hours later. Holly saw that too, and gained little comfort from the warning that the cyclone was still moving south and eastward, but slowly.

Saturday was the longest day in her life. Only half

awake, but too tense to sleep, she prowled the house like a zombie, the radio blaring constantly and the transistor radio always within reach in case of the power failure she feared.

Outside, the rain was a shimmering curtain, a drab and yet somehow magical curtain that filled everything with its presence. The very air was saturated; it was like moving through a steam bath. And the parched, arid red soil had long since lost all ability to absorb the moisture. Runnels of dark red water scoured through the garden, built to rivulets in the gutters and spread into bloody sheets across the roads.

But only the rain was constant. Cyclone Wade was displaying all the unpredictability of his breed, first veering to the north, then swinging south again. Every cyclone warning was different, and the cyclone was at least twelve hours away.

There was some small consolation in seeing two men across the street, soaked and fumbling as they struggled with their cyclone shutters in the drenching downpour. At least, Holly thought, she'd been spared that by her earlier planning.

It wasn't until early afternoon that she first noticed the winds. Mild at first, merely tendrils that flung the grey raindrops from their perpendicular descent. But by evening they were no longer light, having matured to shrieking demons that hammered at the windows and flung themselves against the house with increasing violence.

There was a tangible tension now in the voice of the radio announcer reading the cyclone warnings. But his tension was nothing compared to Holly's own. She was so over-tired, so keyed up with worry that she spooked at every noise, shied at every change in the pressure of the winds.

And the winds continued into the night, growing as Cyclone Wade, according to the radio, smashed across

the coast a good hundred kilometres north of Port
Hedland, then turned immediately and spun back out
to sea as if to gather strength for another assault.

And where next time? Holly couldn't make herself
believe anything but the worst, although she mentally
cursed herself for being such a pessimist.

She was never sure when it was that she noticed the
shift in wind direction, but a mighty crashing from the
patio was her first frightening warning. The lounge
chair!

Screaming, first in alarm and then in chastisement at
her own stupidity, Holly dashed to the back door and
flung back the restraining bolts. She hardly noticed the
force with which the door slammed inward, driven by
the winds, nor the force of the storm-blown rain that
instantly drenched both herself and the entire floor
behind her.

All she could think of was getting the lounge chair off
the patio and away from the dangerous forces of the
wind. Stooping, she dashed out into the storm with all
the speed she could muster, fighting the wind for every
step, gasping with the strain and almost drowning as
the rain was blown back into her panting mouth.

In the eerie patio lights, the storm took on new and
ominous dimensions, grew far more fearful than when
viewed from the dry, comparative safety of the house.
Moving at all was like trying to run under water;
finding the twisted remains of the patio lounger was
easy, but moving it was nearly impossible. Even with
the plastic covers torn and flapping, it presented a
viable target for the predatory wind, and the first time
she tried to pick up the jumble of aluminium and plastic,
she gained only a slashing blow across the cheek when
the storm slapped the torn cover into her face.

But she had to get it. She had to! Oblivious now to
her own danger, to the utter foolishness of her efforts,

she snatched at the tangled mess again, this time dragging it slowly along, moving step by sodden step towards the open door and safety.

The wind slapped at her, punching, buffeting, throwing her balance awry, whipping her hair into a sodden, blinding cloud. Once it flung her against the wall so hard she grazed her knuckles; a moment later it flung a broken branch against her leg, sending her sprawling into the wreckage of the lounger.

And it howled! Lord, how it howled. Even dulled by the soaking rain, it screamed into her ears like a migrant banshee, deafening her in a cacophony of sound. It even seemed, for one small instant, to call her name, wailing it out like a voice from the grave.

Ho-o-o-o-o-olly! The sound meant nothing. In her exhaustion, she couldn't be bothered to think about it; she could only continue her struggle with the malignant wreckage of the patio lounger, which she now moved by crawling along the wall on her hands and knees, one elbow thrust through a bend in the aluminium frame of the thing as she dragged it along.

Something struck her arm, lightly. Another branch? She didn't even bother to look, knowing the blinding wind and rain would make it impossible to see anything anyway.

But then something grabbed her, something that clamped solidly to her free arm, lifting her, pulling her upright against the force of the storm. The patio lounger was struck from her grip to smash against the wall and tumble limply as her other arm was grasped. She looked up then, into eyes like green fire, eyes that seemed to draw out the remains of her strength.

The last thing she saw was those eyes, as her world dissolved into a fuzziness that rushed through her, tumbling her into a soft blackness without sound, without sight.

CHAPTER NINE

CONSCIOUSNESS came slowly, tentatively. It seemed to take hours, during which Holly was dimly aware of a soft, gentle, yet somehow accusing voice that fairly chanted at her. Timed, it seemed, to the luxurious touch of hands that massaged her body, scrubbing at her with something soft, dry.

And in the chant were occasional words that struggled for recognition, some of them tender and loving, others distinctly derogatory. It was like the voice of somebody gentling a fractious colt in terms unmelodic yet soothing.

Very fractious, she thought at one point; there were a great many *damns* and *hells*. But there were other words, too, soothing, gentle words. Or was it merely the tone?

Then she felt something soft against her hair, stroking, drying, smoothing the tangle of dark auburn created by the storm.

Storm! Memory seared back, lifting her with a small squeak of amazement as her eyes flew open to find that she couldn't see. Then Wade removed the towel from around her head and pierced her with an angry-loving-exasperated stare.

'You'll be the death of me yet,' he growled without preamble. 'What in the name of heaven were you trying to do—kill yourself?'

'I . . . I . . .' She got no further.

'I've seen some dumb things in my life,' he snapped, 'but you are the . . . the absolute . . .'

This time it was she who interrupted, having

174

suddenly realised she was lying half in his arms. And naked! Holly squealed again, this time in a combination of rage and outrage.

'What do you think you're doing?' She writhed free, trying vainly to cover herself and dismayed to find she hardly had the strength to move at all. When she moved quickly, everything swam before her eyes, but Wade's voice was clear enough.

'I'm drying you off, what do you think I'm doing?' There was a sort of anger still in his voice, but also something else, a quiet, half-hidden chuckle of amusement. 'It'd be pretty difficult to get you dry and leave your modesty wrapped in the wettest clothes I've ever seen,' he chuckled. 'Apart from my own, that is.'

Holly didn't reply. She was too busy still trying to wriggle free of his grasp, all too aware of his touch as he returned to the task of drying her off.

'Damn it—be still.' Neither anger nor chuckle there now, merely the demand of a man used to being obeyed. She stopped struggling, lay quietly as the towel whipped round her head once more.

'That's much better,' said a soft voice through the enveloping folds of towelling. 'Just a bit more, then you can go see about brushing this into something civilised while I go clean up.'

It was becoming just too confusing. 'Where ... what ...' she stammered, only to have her voice stilled by demands that arrived in a tone that brooked no argument.

'Not now. First you get dry, then you get dressed while I can exercise the little self-control I have left. Damned, silly woman. I swear I'd paddle you until you couldn't sit down for a week, except that in your present condition I fear I'd be tempted to find a more ... enjoyable form of punishment.'

His fingers gripped her throat threateningly, then

traced a lingering path from throat to breast. She didn't need to see where they'd go next; her entire body was already tingling as the ribbons of ecstasy moved. She felt his lips touch briefly at one nipple, then the other, touching so lightly it was less a caress than a prelude to a caress, a promise that swelled her nipples in a greedy demand for more. The flame inside her quickened, flowed into a consuming inferno that brought her every erotic sense awake.

'Wade,' she whispered, wanting him to stop, then not to stop, never to stop.

'My God, but you're beautiful.' The folds of the towel muffled his voice, but there was nothing to muffle the ecstasy of his touch as it deliberately aroused her. His lips were moth wings across her breasts, her thighs, following his fingers in an assault so gentle, so perfect, she couldn't have resisted even if she'd wanted to.

Holly thought she'd melt. And as Wade's caresses became more ardent, her fingers began their own journey of exploration. It was a short one; when she realised that he was dressed still in clothing soaked by the storm and his rescue mission, some semblance of sanity returned.

'You're soaking wet!' she cried, whipping the towel from her tousled hair.

'So what? I'm not made of sugar,' he replied, reaching over to pull her close to him again.

'Perhaps, but you could certainly catch your death of cold,' she replied, trying to force him away by thrusting her palms against the clammy wetness of his chest. It was like shoving against a tree. Wade ignored her efforts and pulled her close against him once more.

'I think we're more than capable of keeping each other warm,' he suggested, his breath warm against her ear. It was tempting, oh, so tempting, to believe him, to give herself. And she would have, had not the wind chosen to take a hand in the discussion. With a clatter that would have shattered any romantic mood, a wayward piece of roofing iron smashed against the bedroom window's cyclone screen and hung there for a moment, vibrating with frustration, before it rattled its way down the wall to land with a crash on the ground below.

Both Holly and Wade flinched in instinctive alarm, but it was she who recovered first. Slipping from his loosened grasp, she flung herself off the bed and leapt to where her bathrobe hung. She wriggled into it, and was tying the belt before he could reach her. And her eyes were wide with a mixture of fear and apprehension.

'The cyclone's getting worse,' she said, her voice a whisper against the sudden onslaught of wind that threatened to rip the entire house apart. Wade looked at her silently, his head cocked as he assessed the situation.

'Wind's shifting,' he muttered. 'The damned thing's shifted direction again. But don't worry, little Hollyhock, this house is as safe as any in town, and a lot safer than most. Now trot out and turn the radio up so we'll know what's going on. I'm off to grab a shower while I can and get into something dry.'

She was glad to follow his directions, pleased to be able to leave the enforced intimacy of the bedroom before her fears and her crying physical needs betrayed her even further. And as soon as he was safely in the shower, she quickly flung on a pair of jeans and a shirt. If the cyclone worsened, she didn't intend being huddled with Wade in the bathroom shelter wearing only her robe. That, she decided, would be tempting fate too far.

There was still no new cyclone warning when he emerged, wet hair tousled, but dressed in khaki trousers and shirt. Almost, she thought, as if he'd had the same thoughts about how they might spend the next few hours.

'Well,' he said with a grin that showed no hint of the mixed emotions Holly felt, 'I guess we're a bit better dressed for it, anyway. Any word yet on what's happening?'

'No,' she replied, and then prattled on as the words flew to her lips. 'How can you possibly be so calm?'

He shrugged. 'Not much else for it. And truly, Holly, you'd do better to relax a bit. Apart from Tracy there haven't been all that many direct hits in all of Australia's history, so I'd give you odds we'll come out of this without too much real damage.'

'Well, I'm sorry,' she replied. 'But I just can't take it quite that calmly.'

Again he shrugged, this time with a wry gleam in his eye. 'You seemed calm enough when I found you outside trying to rescue a patio lounger that was long past saving.'

'I wasn't a bit calm. I was scared stiff,' she said. 'But I was worried it might be blown away and cause damage. That would have been my fault, you see, because I left it out there, and I should have known better.'

'So you should, but I wouldn't worry about it too much. There'll be worse trash than that flying around the town about now. What worries me is how casually you put yourself at risk. I thought I'd have heart failure when I got back to find you outside in that!'

'Well, I didn't particularly enjoy the experience myself,' Holly retorted. 'But there didn't seem to be much else I could do, under the circumstances.'

Wade nodded sagely. 'It was a very brave, selfless and totally stupid act,' he said. 'I'm not really surprised; Jessica might have done the same. I don't know what it is about your family that produced such strong-willed women.'

'I'm sure Jessica would have had more sense than to leave the thing out there in the first place,' Holly replied, ignoring the rest of his comment in her surprise at the unexpected compliment. 'I should have had, too, but I didn't. And besides,' she added, stifling a yawn, 'I was . . .'

'You were half asleep, I suspect,' he said gently. 'I expect you were up all night worrying. Certainly looks like it, from the preparations you've made. Makes me wonder if you were preparing for a simple little cyclone or the next great flood. We could live for a month on what you've stockpiled in the bathroom.'

'I was only doing what your damned emergency pamphlets said I should,' she snapped, growing angry at the criticism.

'Oh, don't get stroppy,' he grinned. 'Nobody's criticising you, and least of all me.' Unexpectedly, he stepped forward to take her shoulders in his great hands, pulling her close so that he could stare into her eyes at close range.

'Are you always like this when you're over-tired?' he asked with a surprising gentleness that didn't quite serve to calm her.

'All you ever do is pick on me,' Holly replied, being quite irrational and knowing she was, but unable to halt her runaway tongue. 'You've criticised me from the very moment you first met me; you've never believed me, never trusted me . . .'

Tears flooded away the rest of what she was going to say, and perhaps just as well, since she didn't know what she was saying anyway. Fatigue and nervous tension had finally taken their toll. Wade, in any event, didn't answer. He just stood, holding her gently and looking down at her with what—from anyone else—she might have taken for genuine compassion.

Then the radio interrupted, and both their attentions

were immediately claimed by the pronouncement that the cyclone had once again turned for the coast, and this time was expected to strike land even further north than before. Also, Wade was now inexplicably weakening.

'Right! That'll be the end of it, then,' Wade growled, releasing Holly as if it were a great effort to do so. 'So for you, young lady, it's bedtime and no arguments. I'll be here if anything new happens, although I'm sure the worst of it's done. I hope so, because I'd hate for us to miss our flight in the morning.'

'In the morning?' Holly couldn't at first credit his words; her sense of timing was as distorted as the rest of her.

'Yes, tomorrow,' he grinned. 'It is, in case you hadn't noticed in your weakened condition, now Sunday morning—if only just. And tomorrow morning we catch our flight, cyclone or no cyclone—provided the planes are going, of course.'

And taking her again by the shoulders, he steered her gently but firmly towards her bedroom, walking her along as if she were a child past its bedtime.

'Right—into the sack with you,' he said. 'Can't have you flying to Perth with great bags under your eyes. Jessica'd have my hide for not taking proper care of our little treasure.'

'But, what about you?' she replied. And then finally managed to voice the question that had been brewing in her mind ever since she'd recovered to find him there. 'How did you get here? There couldn't have been any aircraft flying in that!'

'What kind of a silly question is that?' he replied, and managed to look genuinely puzzled.

'Not at all silly,' said Holly, but less certainly, now, less sure of herself. Could she really have been mistaken? Could it possibly be that he hadn't been in Perth with Ramona?

'Well, it's silly to me. I don't think you're tracking properly,' he said. 'Now please, just go to bed. I've spent eighteen hours getting here and I'm in no mood to play silly games, so just go to sleep like a good little girl and we'll talk about it in the morning. This is no time to be a nuisance and you're too tired anyway.'

Nuisance! The word flew around inside her brain like some evil spirit during the forty-five seconds it took her to realise he was right. She was too tired to be arguing something she was so unsure of. And the word was first into her head when she emerged from exhausted sleep more than twelve hours later.

Nuisance! Yes, she decided, that was exactly the problem. To Wade she was only a nuisance, and could never be anything else. So why bother to discuss last night's question? It just didn't matter, and never would.

She walked quietly through to the kitchen and put the coffee on, then sat staring out into the lifting dawn, marvelling at the nearly cloudless sky, the light, nearly normal breeze.

'It's almost as if it never happened,' she mused, although there was sufficient evidence in the form of wind-strewn rubbish and surface water to reveal that she hadn't totally imagined the cyclone.

'Oh, it happened all right.' The voice from behind her caused Holly to turn with a start, but Wade showed no interest in her surprise. 'Luckily, good old Wade blew himself out almost immediately after crossing the coast the second time,' he said. 'Is this coffee for me? Good planning, dear Holly, because this morning I need it more than you can imagine.'

He joined her at the table, explaining in general terms how he'd been out most of the afternoon before and all night—while she slept, Holly realised, although he didn't mention that—helping to clean up the wind damage in the town.

'I must congratulate you on how you handled yourself,' he said. 'There were a lot of people in town who didn't do nearly so well—ignoring the foolhardy rescue of the patio lounger—and there was a lot of quite unneccessary damage.'

Holly was barely listening, her mind still trying to accept the abrupt disappearance of the cyclone. 'But, you mean it's over? Just like that?' she asked, turning to stare out the window.

'Just like that. Except for the mopping up,' he said. 'Hard to believe, isn't it? The main centre of the cyclone missed by a fair bit, and where it crossed the coast there wasn't much for it to hurt anyway. I expect the roads will be cut for a few days, and there'll be trees knocked down, but that's nothing very serious.'

'It is hard to believe,' she admitted. 'I expected, well, I'm not really sure. The pamphlets don't deal as much with the aftermath, but while it was on it just seemed as if it would go on forever.'

'And you were a lot more frightened than you let on,' Wade replied. 'Not that I blame you for that; so was I. But now I can assure you that Wade is out of your life forever. Gone, blown out and finished.'

Too true, Holly thought. Or at least, almost true. Certainly she must accept that as soon as Jessica was recovered, Wade would indeed be out of her life.

That thought was sufficient to put a damper on her mood, and it was a damper that remained during their trip to the airport and throughout the long flight south. Coupled with that was the question of facing Jessica, who by this time might be expecting a blast for having deceived them so badly, but even so, Jessica couldn't help but be alert to Holly's reaction to Wade. What might she say? And worse, what could Holly reply without making matters worse?

She also didn't know how her aunt would react to the

fact that they'd just *left* the house! Wade, under Holly's questioning, had blithely dismissed the issue—as being of no importance, and had then refused to discuss it further.

And throughout the flight, he'd seemed as moody and withdrawn as Holly, staring out the window through most of the journey and speaking only when absolutely necessary.

When they arrived in Perth, he ignored the hired car outlet and instead dragged Holly towards the taxi rank, where he brusquely commandeered the first available cab and directed her inside.

But it was not to the hospital that he directed the driver; it was to the self-same flat they'd shared on Holly's arrival from Britain.

'What are you doing?' Holly demanded, confused and becoming angry herself in reflection of Wade's mood. How could he possibly contemplate visiting Jessica with them both so angry and disturbed?

'I'm taking you somewhere we can talk privately,' was the blunt reply. 'Now just sit quietly and do as you're told.'

'I will not!' Holly cried, loudly enough to draw the cab driver's attention. The man turned to glare at Wade accusingly, only to grin when Wade turned on his charm and winked at him.

'She's suffering a bit from pre-wedding jitters,' he said with a broad grin. 'She'll be all right once we get some place private, if you know what I mean.'

The driver grinned, and Holly was stunned into silence at the cunningness of the ploy. How could he dare say such a thing? Or was this something worse, some beginning of a plot to make Jessica feel better, to help speed her recovery?

By the time she'd worked out that much, it was too late to argue. The driver pulled up at the flat, and Wade had both Holly and their luggage into the lift before she could argue.

She followed him meekly into the flat, flinching at the mixture of angry, hurtful and delightfully sensuous memories.

Wade said, 'Sit!' and she did so, perched on the edge of her chair like some frightened bird, mesmerised by the eye of her personal cobra, but unable to flee.

'Right,' he said. 'Do you want a drink first, or shall we get on with this?'

'On with what?' she cried, but he wasn't listening.

'A drink, first, I think. Lord knows I need one. Holly, you are the most frustrating, annoying, totally unpredictable woman I have ever met.' And he continued to mutter to himself as he poured their drinks and brought hers over.

'Now,' he said in a voice like silk over steel. 'What was all this nonsense the other night about how did I get there? And don't trouble to try and gloss it over, because I know it must have been damned important to you for it to come up under such stressful circumstances and I intend to have some very straight answers.'

She tried to be evasive despite the warning, but his insistent probing quickly revealed at least the reason for her query, Ramona's phone call. Holly managed, quite successfully, she thought, to evade mentioning her own immediate interpretation of the thing.

Wade sipped at his drink, his pale eyes holding her to silence until he replied. 'And of course you thought I'd done the dirty on you, and gone off to Perth, leaving you to cope with the cyclone on your own, along with everything else. Ah, Holly, I'd really have expected you to think better of me than that.'

'I . . .' She paused. What sense to deny it? She couldn't lie to him without him knowing it immediately.

'Well just so you know,' he said, 'I got there by

driving for eighteen hours in something less than ideal driving conditions, breaking Lord knows how many laws in the process. But yes, I did see Ramona, whom I imagine deliberately set out to get you going. I was in the process of closing out the last of my business associations with her father, and she flew up with him that same day—and back again, I might add.'

Again, he paused to observe Holly, speculation ripe in his eyes. 'And if I didn't know better, dear Holly, I'd think you were not only suspicious of me, but jealous into the bargain. Were you?' The final words were soft, intent.

'No, of course not,' Holly managed to reply, lying quite brazenly.

'Just as well. I cannot *abide* jealous women,' Wade said, almost smugly. 'And you realise, I expect, that it was Ramona's jealousy of *you* that caused her to deliberately lead you into thinking what you did? Not to mention, of course, that ridiculous gambit of using an English accent to order all that glassware for the party.'

'I . . . I don't think I want to talk about this,' Holly managed to say. 'And it doesn't matter anyway; it's all in the past.'

'Too right it is, and just for the record, so is Ramona, who has had no significant part in my life since well before you came into it,' Wade said. 'Now is there anything else you'd like straightened out? If so, out with it, because I'm damned if I'm going to have shadows hanging over my head when I propose to you.'

'When you what?' Holly couldn't believe what she'd heard.

'Just what I said. We are not going to see Jessica until we can tell her we're getting married as soon as she's well enough to join us in church. Much as it hurts me to admit her matchmaking worked, *had* worked, in fact, before you even got to Australia. Damn it, Holly, I think I must have fallen in love with you just from your picture and your letters.'

Holly sat there, the glass unnoticed in her fingers as she stared at Wade. She wanted to answer him, to declare her own feelings, but the words wouldn't come.

And yet the answer was there, in her eyes and in her heart, and when Wade reached out to pull her into his arms, he could read it well enough. And then she could say it, oblivious to the spilled drink she'd dropped.

'I didn't have a picture to fall in love with,' she whispered. 'And I don't think you could have . . .' The rest was lost when his lips drowned out her words, magically banishing every fear she'd ever had, every doubt.

'I just can't understand how you took so long to see it,' he said after an endless moment. 'I realise that I didn't come right out and tell you that I loved you; but I thought you must be able to see it. If we hadn't been interrupted at Honeymoon Cove you'd have known, that's for sure.'

'Only if you'd told me,' Holly replied. 'I was so sure you couldn't love me, after that incident in the airport and all the misinterpretations *that* caused.'

'Only in your own mind,' he whispered. 'I'd forgotten it long ago, or would have if you hadn't kept bringing it up. But I'm telling you now, Holly. I love you. And I'll keep right on telling you, because we've had enough misinterpretations to last us a lifetime.'

And there was nothing to misinterpret in the kiss he gave her then, no room for anything but the bliss of their togetherness, the fusing of their emotions as she returned the kiss eagerly.

It was a kiss that lasted an instant, an hour, a lifetime, scorching and yet infinitely gentle, scalding and yet also infinitely cool and wonderful. And over far too soon, for Holly's taste.

'We might just have time to go find you an engagement ring before we go off to the hospital,' Wade said finally, his eyes now alive with the love she returned. 'Or would you mind visiting Jessica without one—until tomorrow?'

'I'm not sure,' Holly laughed. 'What would we do instead?'

His hand slid down to cup her breast, fingertips aglow with that special magic that only Wade's fingers could ever have for her. She felt her body respond, cry out for more of his caresses. She laughed, joyous in a world so full, so overflowing with everything she wanted and needed.

'We'd better buy the ring now,' she said. 'There isn't time for what you've got in mind.'

'Oh, yes, there is,' he purred in her ear, one arm pulling her even closer against him.

And there was!

Coming Next Month in Harlequin Romances!

2731 TEARS OF GOLD Helen Conrad
The mystery man found panning for gold on a young woman's
California estate sparks her imagination—especially when she learns
he's bought her family home!

2732 LORD OF THE AIR Carol Gregor
There's turbulence ahead when the owner of a flying school wants
to build a runway on his neighbor's land. He disturbs her privacy,
not to mention her peace of mind....

2733 SPRING AT SEVENOAKS Miriam MacGregor
A young Englishwoman's visit to a New Zealand sheep station
arouses the owner's suspicions. No woman could be counted on to
live in such isolation! Why should she be any different?

2734 WEDNESDAY'S CHILD Leigh Michaels
Is it generosity that prompts a man to offer his estranged wife money
for their son's medical expenses? Or is it a bid to get her under his
thumb again?

2735 WHERE THE GODS DWELL Celia Scott
A fashion photographer abandons her glamorous career for an
archaeological dig in Crete. But she has second thoughts when she
falls in love...and clashes with old-world Greece.

2736 WILDERNESS BRIDE Gwen Westwood
Concern brings an estranged wife to her husband's side on an
African wilderness reserve when blindness threatens him. But he
insists on reconquering the wilderness...and her!

You're invited to accept 4 books and a surprise gift Free!

Acceptance Card

Mail to: Harlequin Reader Service®

In the U.S.
2504 West Southern Ave.
Tempe, AZ 85282

In Canada
P.O. Box 2800, Postal Station A
5170 Yonge Street
Willowdale, Ontario M2N 6J3

YES! Please send me 4 free Harlequin American Romance® novels and my free surprise gift. Then send me 4 brand new novels as they come off the presses. Bill me at the low price of $2.25 each —an 11% saving off the retail price. There are no shipping, handling or other hidden costs. There is no minimum number of books I must purchase. I can always return a shipment and cancel at any time. Even if I never buy another book from Harlequin, the 4 free novels and the surprise gift are mine to keep forever.

154 BPA-BPGE

Name	(PLEASE PRINT)

Address	Apt. No.

City	State/Prov.	Zip/Postal Code

This offer is limited to one order per household and not valid to present subscribers. Price is subject to change.　　　ACAR-SUB-1

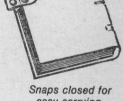

Take 4 books & a surprise gift FREE

SPECIAL LIMITED-TIME OFFER

Mail to   **Harlequin Reader Service**®

In the U.S.
2504 West Southern Ave.
Tempe, AZ 85282

In Canada
P.O. Box 2800, Station "A"
5170 Yonge Street
Willowdale, Ontario M2N 6J3

YES! Please send me 4 free Harlequin Romance® novels and my free surprise gift. Then send me 6 brand-new novels every month as they come off the presses. Bill me at the low price of $1.65 each ($1.75 in Canada)—a 11% saving off the retail price. There are no shipping, handling or other hidden costs. There is no minimum number of books I must purchase. I can always return a shipment and cancel at any time. Even if I never buy another book from Harlequin, the 4 free novels and the surprise gift are mine to keep forever.

Name   (PLEASE PRINT)

Address   Apt. No.

City   State/Prov.   Zip/Postal Code

This offer is limited to one order per household and not valid to present subscribers. Price is subject to change.   DOR–SUB–1

Experience the warmth of ...

Harlequin Romance

**The original romance novels.
Best-sellers for more than 30 years.**

Delightful and intriguing love stories
by the world's foremost writers
of romance fiction.

Be whisked away to dazzling
international capitals ...
or quaint European villages.
Experience the joys of falling in love ...
for the first time, the best time!

Harlequin Romance

**A uniquely absorbing journey
into a world of superb romance reading.**

Wherever paperback books are sold, or through
Harlequin Reader Service

In the U.S.	In Canada
2504 West Southern Avenue	P.O. Box 2800, Postal Station A
Tempe, AZ 85282	5170 Yonge Street
	Willowdale, Ontario M2N 6J3

**No one touches the heart of a woman
quite like Harlequin!**

R-111